YA
362.29
STE

B2029563 37

B2029563 7

THE other AMERICA

Teen ADDICTS

These and other titles are included in *The Other America* series:

Battered Women	People with AIDS
Gangs	Teen Dropouts
Gay and Lesbian Youth	Teen Fathers
The Homeless	Teen Mothers
Homeless Teens	Teen Runaways
Illegal Immigrants	Teens in Prison

THEotherAMERICA

Teen ADDICTS

by
Gail B. Stewart

Photographs by
Carl Franzén

Lucent Books, P.O. Box 289011, San Diego, CA 92198-9011

Cover design: Carl Franzén

Library of Congress Cataloging-in-Publication Data
Stewart, Gail, 1949–
    Teen addicts / by Gail B. Stewart; photographs by Carl Franzén.
      p. cm. — (The Other America)
    Includes bibliographical references (p.   ) and index.
    Summary: Provides an overview of drug addiction, describes the lives of four teenage drug addicts, and suggests ways to get involved in fighting this social problem.
    ISBN 1-56006-574-5 (lib. bdg. : alk. paper)
    1. Teenagers—Drug use—United States Case studies Juvenile literature.   2. Narcotic addicts—United States Biography Juvenile literature.   3. Drug abuse—United States Case studies Juvenile literature. [1. Drug abuse.]   I. Franzén, Carl, ill.   II. Title.   III. Series: Stewart, Gail, 1949–   Other America.
HV5809.5.S84   2000
362.29'0835'092273—dc21   99-20820
                                                                                          CIP

The opinions of and stories told by the people in this book are entirely their own. The author has presented their accounts in their own words and has not verified their accuracy. Thus, the author can make no claim as to the objectivity of their accounts.

No part of this book may be reproduced or used in any form or by any means, electrical, mechanical, or otherwise, including, but not limited to, photocopy, recording, or any information storage and retrieval system, without prior written permission from the publisher.

                      Printed in the U.S.A.
              Copyright © 2000 by Lucent Books, Inc.
         P.O. Box 289011, San Diego, CA 92198-9011

Contents

FOREWORD	6
INTRODUCTION	8
The Facts About Teen Addicts	

TYRONE 14
At nineteen, Tyrone's life has been marred by hardships and poor choices. Although he would like to better himself, Tyrone seems unable to accept responsibility for his actions and unwilling to give up his addiction to marijuana.

TESHINDA 36
After a year of sobriety, seventeen-year-old Teshinda is optimistic about her future and realistic about her past. Although she was sexually abused as a child, Teshinda accepts responsibility for both her addiction and her destructive behavior.

JORGE 59
Crippled by polio and living in an adopted family, Jorge has been haunted by emotional problems. Today, the nineteen-year-old former marijuana addict is regretful of his past and the rift it has caused in his family.

JODI 83
Fifteen-year-old Jodi, a marijuana addict, comes from a home shattered by violence and drug abuse. Consequently, she seems unable to comprehend the seriousness of her addiction and its devastating consequences.

EPILOGUE	103
WAYS YOU CAN GET INVOLVED	105
FOR FURTHER READING	107
INDEX	108
ABOUT THE AUTHOR	111
ABOUT THE PHOTOGRAPHER	112

Foreword

O, YES,
I SAY IT PLAIN,
AMERICA NEVER WAS AMERICA TO ME.
AND YET I SWEAR THIS OATH—
AMERICA WILL BE!
> LANGSTON HUGHES

Perhaps more than any other nation in the world, the United States represents an ideal to many people. The ideal of equality—of opportunity, of legal rights, of protection against discrimination and oppression. To a certain extent, this image has proven accurate. But beneath this ideal lies a less idealistic fact—many segments of our society do not feel included in this vision of America.

They are the outsiders—the homeless, the elderly, people with AIDS, teenage mothers, gang members, prisoners, and countless others. When politicians and the media discuss society's ills, the members of these groups are defined as what's wrong with America; they are the people who need fixing, who need help, or increasingly, who need to take more responsibility. And as these people become society's fix-it problem, they lose all identity as individuals and become part of an anonymous group. In the media and in our minds these groups are identified by condition—a disease, crime, morality, poverty. Their condition becomes their identity, and once this occurs, in the eyes of society, they lose their humanity.

The Other America series reveals the members of these groups as individuals. Through in-depth interviews, each person tells his or her unique story. At times these stories are painful, revealing individuals who are struggling to maintain their integrity, their humanity, their lives, in the face of fear, loss, and economic and spiritual hardship. At other times, their tales are exasperating, demonstrating a litany of poor choices, shortsighted thinking, and self-gratification. Nevertheless, their identities remain distinct, their personalities diverse.

As we listen to the people of *The Other America* series describe their experiences, they cease to be stereotypically defined and become tangible, individual. In the process, we may begin to understand more profoundly and think more critically about society's problems. When politicians debate, for example, whether the homeless problem is due to a poor economy or lack of initiative, it will help to read the words of the homeless. Perhaps then we can see the issue more clearly. The family who finds itself temporarily homeless because it has always been one paycheck from poverty is not the same as the mother of six who has been chronically chemically dependent. These people's circumstances are not all of one kind, and perhaps we, after all, are not so very different from them. Before we can act to solve the problems of the Other America, we must be willing to look down their path, to see their faces. And perhaps in doing so, we may find a piece of ourselves as well.

Introduction

THE FACTS ABOUT TEEN DRUG ADDICTS

Marty is a sixteen-year-old Chicago boy who has used drugs since he was ten. He figures that he has been addicted for six years.

"I started with pot," he says. "It is so easy to get at school, in my neighborhood, from pretty much all the older kids I know. And after doing that a while, some of my friends were huffing, you know? Like they'd take a rag and spray oven cleaner or paint thinner or something on it, and just inhale. That was even easier, because you didn't have to buy the stuff; it's in everybody's house. And the high off that is good. And from huffing—I don't know. We just tried whatever drug people had. Sometimes it would be crank, or acid, or speed.

"I know I'm addicted," he continues. "I used to pretend that I wasn't, that I could quit anytime I wanted to. But it's too hard to stop. Getting high is what I like best of all; it's all I ever think about."

"IT SCARES ME A LOT"

Minnesota youth worker Kara Sherman has seen plenty of Martys over the past twenty-two years. She warns that the number of substance abusers has been increasing, especially over the last few years.

"It's very strange," she says. "When I was just out of college in the '70s, the use of drugs like speed, LSD, and amphetamines was prevalent—that was the time right on the heels of 'flower power' and all that. After that, things slowed down; we had a backlash against the whole '70s drug lifestyle, and in the '80s there was 'Just say no,' courtesy of Nancy Reagan.

"But now in 1998 we're hearing studies that show that the drug use—and the addiction that accompanies it—is skyrocketing again.

I personally am seeing lots more kids on crank, on crack cocaine [which didn't exist in the '60s], on acid, and on speed—not to mention marijuana! One of the parents on our school board asked me the other day if this increase doesn't give me reason for concern. I told him, 'Concern isn't even the appropriate word. It scares me a lot!'"

GRIM STATISTICS

The recent statistics alarm many people who work with teenagers. One 1996 survey by the U.S. Department of Health and Human Services found that abuse of illicit drugs, primarily marijuana, among teens between the ages of twelve and seventeen has more than doubled since 1992, after years of decline.

Another study by the University of Michigan in 1997 highlights the prevalence of drug use by age bracket. More than 40 percent of high school seniors, for example, admitted to using illegal drugs in the past twelve months. Drug users accounted for 38 percent of tenth graders. And 24 percent of eighth graders said that they had used illegal drugs in the past year.

As a result of increased substance abuse by today's teens, emergency rooms are busier treating overdoses, treatment centers are busier trying to help addicted teens deal with their problems, and counselors and social workers are busier assisting families whose very essence has been destroyed by drugs.

"These are the hardest battles of all," says one adolescent psychologist. "There are no statistics that can show the number of young lives messed up by getting high instead of going to school, or dropping out of after-school athletic programs to hang out with the neighborhood burnouts. The little, day-to-day decisions made by drugged adolescents can haunt them the rest of their lives."

"Experts" are not alone in their concern; indeed, according to a 1995 survey by Columbia University's Center on Addiction and Substance Abuse, 32 percent of high school students interviewed believed that drugs were by far the biggest problem they face—outranking sex, grades, peer pressure, and crime.

WHY DOES IT HAPPEN?

Teens are turning to drugs today more than in recent years for a variety of reasons. For one thing, experts cite the ways in which popular culture glamorizes drug use.

"It's in the music our kids hear, and the videos they watch," says one drug counselor. "Back in the '80s for a while it was even a part of the fashion world—shirts, hats, wallets, jackets adorned with the marijuana leaf. And the message is not so subtle: Drug use is cool."

Ginna Marston, a director of the Partnership for a Drug-Free America, agrees. "Teenagers today receive fewer warnings and more positive messages about drugs," she says, "especially those coming from popular culture. Music, media, and fashion have a profound influence on the way young people see the world around them. And what they're seeing is a world that increasingly tells them that smoking pot is fun, cool, inconsequential, and a normal part of growing up."

"I Figured, What Could It Hurt?"

Peer pressure is another factor that accounts for widespread drug abuse among teens. Being around friends who urge you to try drugs is a difficult situation, say young people.

"I was always hanging around these two kids at my school," says Darrin, an addict who began smoking marijuana in fifth grade. "It was like, if I didn't do stuff with those guys, then I'd be alone. So I went along with them, when they fired up a joint one day. I figured, what could it hurt? By saying no, I would have been cut off, so I didn't."

One of the commonly cited reasons teens give for using drugs is that the high provides an escape from the unpleasantness of their lives. Many teens complain about the excessive demands made upon them by teachers, parents, and coaches.

"All my dad could ever talk about was me making the honor roll so I could get into the college *he* went to," says eighteen-year-old Brandon, a former addict. "It got so that I just wanted to get away. And buying a hit of acid for five bucks and then putting the earphones on and zoning out in my room was the easiest way."

Those most vulnerable to drug abuse come from single-parent homes often complicated by instability and violence. A three-hour acid trip or even a short high from smoking marijuana can provide a temporary escape from their lives, too.

Teshinda, one of the young people interviewed for *The Other America: Teen Addicts*, was sexually assaulted by her mother's boyfriend over a period of years. The seventeen-year-old recalls finding that using inhalants and marijuana became the only ways she could cope.

"It made me feel like I fit in, in ways I'd never felt before," she remembers. "I was calm, relaxed. I felt like I could always say the right thing, or be silent when that was cool, too. I was a different person. I wasn't the girl who'd been abused. I was better—I was popular—I was at peace."

Fourteen-year-old Mara concurs. "My mom and dad were always fighting—from the second they got home from work. I'd go over to my friend Norah's house; her sister had a stash of weed. I liked how it made me feel—all giggly and silly. I didn't think about being scared that my parents would get a divorce. While I was high, I didn't even care."

THE "GATEWAY" DRUG

Perhaps the most insidious of the illegal drugs today is the most common—marijuana. It is what drug counselors call a "gateway" drug, for it often leads to the use of other drugs. So high is that probability that a 1995 report by the Center on Addiction and Substance Abuse concluded that youth between twelve and seventeen who have used marijuana are eighty-five times more likely to use cocaine than those who have never used it.

The drug is insidious in other ways. For instance, its reputation among aging baby boomers recalling its use in the '60s and '70s is fairly benign. Parents today often tend to be less concerned about a son or daughter experimenting with marijuana, thinking, "I smoked a little pot in college—no big deal."

"My mom and dad smoke weed sometimes—I can smell it in their bedroom," says one middle-class teen. "For the longest time they denied it, but I finally said, 'God—do you think I'm stupid? Don't you think I can recognize that smell?' So they finally admitted it, that they get a little high once in a while. But then they have the nerve to tell me that they're old enough to handle it. My mom says, 'If I ever catch *you* smoking pot, there'll be hell to pay!' But the way I look at it, if they can do it, why can't I?"

Those parents who minimize the drug's effects are often unaware how different marijuana of the '90s is from that of the '60s and '70s. Experts say that today's drug is up to ten times more potent—and more addictive.

THE PATH TO ADDICTION

Not everyone who uses drugs is addicted to them. Some define their own use as "experimentation" or "just being curious." However, many teens find out the hard way that casual usage can turn to addiction without warning.

Nineteen-year-old Joe found that after trying crank once, he was hopelessly dependent on it. "Maybe I just have a brain that gets addicted easy, I don't know," he says. "But that's all I could think about, after using that one time. From the time I got up till I went to bed, doing crank was the only thing that seemed important. I'd lie, steal, do whatever it took to get my next hit."

Drug counselors agree that many youths underestimate the power of addiction, believing that they are invincible. "I've got teenage clients who are stoned ten or twelve hours a day," says one. "You ask them about their addiction, and they'll look at you like you're from the moon. They say, 'I'm not addicted. I can stop this anytime I want.' They don't even know how dependent on drugs they are."

Though the process of addiction varies, experts cite several general behaviors that may indicate a teen's dependence on drugs. A sudden change in mood or attitude or an abrupt lack of interest in activities that once were pleasurable are common signs of addiction. Teen addicts frequently start skipping school, stealing, or lying about their whereabouts. They may experience a noticeable loss of weight or unexplained bouts of depression. Such behaviors indicate cause for concern by family, friends, or teachers.

FOUR ADDICTS

The four teens interviewed in *The Other America: Teen Addicts* tell very different stories of their own addictions. Tyrone, a black teen from Milwaukee, was raised by parents who were addicted to crack. He has not sought treatment or help for his dependence on marijuana, even though he readily admits he is addicted. "I'm fine the way I am," he says with a smile. "I don't hurt anybody, and it's not like I'm doing cocaine or something that can kill me. So who cares?"

Teshinda, seventeen, was addicted to inhalants and marijuana until she went through treatment. She believes that until the addict herself wants to change, all the treatment in the world won't help. "My life was a mess," she confides, "and the drugs were just part of it. It's like, I couldn't successfully deal with my addiction until I got help for my depression and my anger. And until I myself was ready, nobody could help me—not foster homes, not shelters, not hospitals, not treatment centers. It was all inside me."

At fifteen, Jodi has been addicted to acid, speed, and marijuana. "Weed is definitely the most addictive for me," she admits. "I could give up speed and acid forever, but weed is another story." She says that she "might want to go through treatment someday," but that it will be hard, since there is a great deal of drug using going on within her home.

Jorge, nineteen, considers himself cured of his addiction to acid and marijuana. Adopted by an upper-middle-class American family when he was a baby in Colombia, he struggled with being the only minority in the wealthy suburb where he lived. He believes his substance abuse was triggered by anger and resentment toward his parents—most of it unwarranted, he admits. "My main motivation for getting past my addiction was my family," he explains. "I did a lot of things when I was addicted that I'm ashamed of; I stole and lied to my parents. It's not a time of my life that I'm proud of at all."

Tyrone

> "THE REST [OF MY FAMILY] ARE DOPE FIENDS, ALL INTO CRACK. THEY'VE BEEN DOING IT SO LONG, I DON'T THINK THEY REMEMBER WHEN THEY *WEREN'T* DOING IT. IT SEEMS LIKE NOTHING EVER CHANGES IN OUR FAMILY, EXCEPT FOR THE WORSE."

Author's Note: Nineteen-year-old Tyrone is a self-described drug addict from Milwaukee, Wisconsin. Because he uses a great deal of marijuana, it is not surprising that he is unreliable about keeping appointments for interviews and photography sessions. Although he is friendly and engaging, he seems unreasonable at times, blaming others for his own weaknesses and shortcomings—such as his lack of a job.

Inside, sitting over a cup of hot coffee, Tyrone is still shivering in his gray pullover sweater.

"Man, I been standing in the doorway of that video place," he says. "I thought I could get out of that wind, but it's a killer. I'll tell you, I should be used to this weather; I grew up in Milwaukee, and they got cold just like this. Colder, maybe, because we're right on the lake. But I can't get warm, now. I guess it's time to find a coat."

Tyrone is slender and seems younger than his nineteen years. He smiles. He tends to stutter a bit, especially when talking about himself.

"I'm from Milwaukee," he starts. "I just come up from there about eight months ago. I've been staying a lot of places, but lately just in shelters and stuff—except I hope that things will be changing for me for the better.

"I'm an addict, yeah. I guess I consider myself an alcoholic, too. I don't mean that I'm loaded or drunk every minute, because I'm not. But I feel like I need the drugs or I need the booze to function the way I like to function. I ain't never been in treatment. I don't need to be, that's why. I'm okay the way I am, and I don't need anybody telling me different."

FAMILY IN MILWAUKEE

Tyrone grew up in one of the poorest sections of Milwaukee's north side.

"We was in a ghetto," he says without emotion. "We lived on a street called Fond du Lac. My mom never had a job; she got welfare. My dad didn't work too much, either. See, he had a bullet in his back from back when he was a young man, and he can't do too much now. Once in a while he'd get a temporary job, like maybe at a car wash or something. But mostly it was nothing."

Tyrone laughs a little when asked if his father's injury was war related.

"Yeah, maybe if you mean *street* wars," he says. "He was in a gang back in the seventies. That was before there was Vice Lords or Gangster Disciples or anything like that. It was just territorial stuff, you know? Anyway, he got shot two times in one of those fights, and stabbed a couple of times, too."

He smiles briefly.

"I been following in my dad's footsteps, you might say. Anyway, I got a brother Clifton. He's three years younger than me—he's like fifteen now, close to sixteen. He's still down there with them in Milwaukee. Not in school, no. He's trying to follow in *my* footsteps, I guess. That's not the best idea for him, you know? But that's what he's doing. It's his life. He's drinking, smoking weed, breaking into people's houses. Just like what I was doing back there."

PARENTS AS ROLE MODELS

Asked if he misses his family in Milwaukee, Tyrone has to think about his answer.

"In a way," he says slowly. "I mean, I love my parents, because they're my parents, they brought me up. But what they're doing is bad. They're on drugs, on crack. They been on it for years, I know that. They drink, smoke crack, and it's cost them their rent money. Now they're out on the streets; they got nowhere to go, you know what I'm saying?

"I saw them like two months ago. I was down there. But it was so bad—I don't want to be going back there. Nothing's ever going to change; they'll be doing those drugs forever, man."

Tyrone says that the onset of his parents' drug use is not recent.

"They been doing the drugs, like smoking pot, back before I was born," he explains. "I'd always watch them, when I was little, you know? They'd go into one of the bedrooms of our house, you know, with their friends. They'd be drinking, you could smell pot. They shut the door, but I knew what they was doing.

"The bad stuff, the crack, didn't start until like '91 or '92, I think. They started sniffing some coke; then they started doing crack all the time. I mean, I didn't know about it at the time. It was because of something I found, something I figured out. And you know how I know about that?"

"I PUT TWO AND TWO TOGETHER"

He smiles. "See, I saw this busted antenna, you know, for a TV set? I wondered what it was. I was like ten or eleven. I saw this silver thing back behind the curtain, on the windowsill. I'm thinking, why keep a busted piece of metal back there? It was like it was important for it to be there, you know? And it was about that time when my mom's talking about not having no money to pay the rent with. Hey, I know we're getting enough, because she's on welfare, right? So all of a sudden, how come we don't have no money? So I put two and two together."

Tyrone notes my puzzled look and explains.

"See, later on, when I was older, I saw a lot of crackheads, dope fiends. Lots of people I knew, relatives. They'd smoke in front of me, man, and one time I seen somebody using an antenna, just like what we got. They used it like a crack pipe, you know? So that's what was going on at my house. That's what my parents were doing. And that's why we got no rent money."

"EVERYBODY KNEW US"

Tyrone says that if it weren't for the crack, his family life might not have been so bad.

"The weed, that was no big deal," he shrugs. "In our neighborhood most everybody drank, did weed. And before '91, like I said before, things weren't so bad. Back then, a lot of our family lived in the same apartment building, you know? On all three floors, we

Tyrone has recently moved away from his family, which seemed to foster his marijuana addiction and dangerous lifestyle.

had like one whole side. All twenty-two of my cousins was there, my six aunts, my uncles—lots of us! And back then, everybody knew us, the whole block. All you had to say was your last name, and they go, 'Man, I know who you are.'"

There was always someone to play with, always something to do, he remembers.

"You'd get off the school bus and your cousins would be waiting, right? You didn't even have to go home first—we didn't bring home no homework, no books, nothing like that. You just take off with your cousins, your friends. You don't have to check in with anybody."

He laughs humorlessly. "I mean, check in with *who?* Who is keeping track?"

His family was forced to move, however, when his parents began spending their rent money on crack.

"It was like this," he says. "She'd owe everybody in the neighborhood, everyone in the family. She'd run out of money—not just for rent, but she'd sell off our food stamps, too. So she'd say, 'Give me twenty dollars and I'll pay you back next check.' But then when the food stamps come, she'd sell them again, and the first thing she'd buy was crack.

"It got to be the same thing every month. She'd have this long list of people she owed. Most of them was family, like I said, so nobody got real mad—I mean, she wasn't into no strangers for it. But the landlord had enough, and our family—my brother and my parents and me—we was out of that building, the one with all of our relatives. That was too bad," he says. "That's when things fell apart for us."

"SCHOOL WAS REAL HARD"

His life at school was not much more pleasant than his home life in those days.

"School was real hard," he says, a little embarrassed. "I'm LD—that's learning disabled. I had trouble learning stuff, and so I had to be in separate classes from most of the other kids. And then they decided I was ED—that's emotionally disturbed. That was because when other kids were horsing around, I couldn't learn.

"My mom found out that if you were ED you could get more welfare money. I'm not sure of why, but she heard about that. The benefits would go up, you know? She wanted to sign me up as ED on there, but when I got older I sort of grew out of those problems—at least the ED part."

By the time he was in middle school, Tyrone's teachers had decided he could handle the work in regular classes. Looking back, however, he says that was a bad decision.

"I was real glad when that happened," he says. "I wanted to be with the other kids. I thought that was cool, hanging with my other friends. But it was hard—the work was too much. I don't know if it was that I couldn't learn or because I wasn't trying too hard, though. See, by that time I was hanging with my gang—my new family."

A New Family

Gang life was as normal in his neighborhood as soccer or Little League teams were in other people's neighborhoods, he says.

"I was always a follower," he admits, smiling. "I mean, when I was like six years old, I'd be wearing my hat to the right, you know, like the boys in the gang. I didn't even know what it was about—I just wanted to look good, right? I didn't know what a GD [Gangster Disciple] was. Just a way to look, that's what it was to me then.

"But after we got kicked out of our old apartment, we moved into this new neighborhood. I was like ten or eleven, I think. Anyway, the kids were all GDs; they asked me to be in the gang, too. I was glad, yeah. I said, sure."

Tyrone met with no objections from his parents on his decision to join the gang.

Following in his father's footsteps, Tyrone joined the Gangster Disciples, the notorious street gang that dominated his Milwaukee neighborhood.

"They knew, yeah," he says. "They knew I was running with those boys. I wore my black and blue, you know. But they didn't say nothing. What are they going to say—I mean, they're too busy doing their own little thing, right? They be sitting home, waiting for their friends to come over with some money, so they can go out and buy some booze, some crack.

"My mama—she can't even do anything in the morning until she's started drinking. That's how she started—she had to. It like—boosted her spirits up, whatever. She and my dad, they were always home, always around. It didn't bother me none, though. Because, see, when I was with the GDs, they were my family. I had no reason to be home.

"We didn't do too much bad stuff then, either. Most of it was fun, really. It was a way of getting into it, learning about how to survive. We'd break into cars, steal stuff out of stores, do some of that. We smoked a little pot, did a little drinking. Not too much at first, but later it was more and more. But that's getting ahead of the story, you know?"

"A Bad Way to Grow Up"

Tyrone says he worried about his younger brother, especially as his parents' drug use increased.

"I wasn't around much," he explains. "And Clifton—he was on his own at home, and there wasn't much to eat. I was making money boosting stuff we stole, so I took care of him. I'd go down to the store, buy us some cold cuts, cheese, bread, stuff like that. Plus, I knew how to cook a few things, like fried chicken. So I'd do that sometimes.

"See, that was a bad way to grow up. I got mad a lot, because things didn't have to be that bad. I wasn't mad that we were poor. We just didn't have to be the way we were, though. I never had things other kids in my neighborhood had—and I ain't talking about designer this and that, no. I'd just wish that I had some clothes that fit. Things would get small, but there'd be no money for bigger pants or a new coat. Or shoes.

"Plus, we'd be wearing the same clothes every day to school, whether they was dirty or not. My mom wasn't washing our clothes, nothing like that. When we lived at that other building, my grandma would come in and clean up our place sometimes. But then she died, and there wasn't nobody interesting in doing that."

Nineteen years old and homeless, Tyrone now lives in temporary shelters—some of which offer shoes and clothing—or stays with friends.

What about holidays, special occasions? Tyrone shakes his head.

"Before crack, Christmas used to be good. We'd have a tree, and lights. Everybody'd come over and help cook—there'd be lots to eat. But the drugs ruined that. It got so we didn't get no tree, nothing. Nobody was cooking. The house was as messy as it always was, and it seemed like nobody noticed. Like I said, it wasn't a good way to grow up—not for me, not for Clifton."

CONTINUING THE CYCLE?

Tyrone's involvement with the gang increased over time, from petty burglaries and shoplifting to more serious crimes, such as drugs—both using and dealing. Does he see some irony in his complaints about his parents' drug use and his own involvement?

"No way," he says emphatically. "I don't consider smoking a little weed, doing some drinking, anything like that, the same as using crack. They're separate things. They were like for relaxation, man—something fun to do.

"I started using when I was ten. I'd go over to my auntie's house—her name is Cookie. She had ten kids, and one of them was my age—Kevin. I think she was getting like a thousand dollars' worth of welfare off of all them kids, you know? She used it all for booze and weed, man. That's what her check went for. Her kids was all dressed from K-Mart and Payless, you know what I mean? Real cheap stuff. But she didn't care—all she liked was the high.

"Anyway, she let us get drunk, get stoned. I liked it fine—I don't think she was a bad person for that. I mean, we weren't getting into trouble; we were safe. I remember in the summertime, we would be over there every day, all day. Cookie didn't care—she was doing it, too. In fact, that's part of why she let us do it, so she had some company while she was getting stoned, you know?"

Tyrone says that his first experience with marijuana was not pleasant.

"It wasn't good the first time I did it," he shrugs. "No big deal for me. I got high, but I didn't like it. I felt paranoid—I felt like someone was coming after me. I was crying, 'cause I thought maybe I'd smoked something else besides weed. It felt like it was a lot stronger than it was supposed to be, you know? I didn't get relaxed, like I was expecting. I remember I was even hiding under the bed, I was so nervous!"

THE DOPE HOUSE

His subsequent experiences with the drug were more pleasant, he says, and by the time he was twelve, Tyrone had become a regular user.

"We'd go to a dope house and smoke weed there," he explains. "Not at home, none of us were spending time at home. I wasn't really hiding it from my parents, though. My mom found out when I was twelve that I was smoking weed. See, I'd come home high, and for once she *wasn't* high. I had the munchies, you know, looking in the drawers and cupboards for something to eat. And plus I was giggling, acting real silly.

"So she says to me, 'Boy, I know what you're doing—I know you're smoking that weed. So I'll tell you it's best for you to do that around here, not out on the street, where something bad could happen to you.' So she wasn't mad. Even if she was, what's she going to do about it? I'm twelve, I'm grown. I don't live there in that house. They can't be telling me nothing, the way I figure it.

"Anyway, the dope house. That's a house that a big-time dope dealer gets. He don't live in it or nothing—he just pays rent, gets furniture from some rental place, a big TV. And he gets some boards to put over the front and back door, so no cops or other gangs can kick them in, you know? And that's where he sells his dope out of. He gets boys in the gang to stay there, do the selling for him.

"That's where we'd drink, get high. I mean, we were in the gang, so we were cool. We'd get a blunt [a cigar filled with marijuana] and smoke it there. We'd get us some booze, too. We'd either get it from kids that were in our gang or we'd see someone going by the liquor store, and we'd ask them to get us something, too. Like get us some Wild Irish Rose, or some Eight Ball, or gin, or whatever we felt like. We'd give the guy a dollar or fifty cents, whatever. Then we'd just sit around inside the dope house, a couple guys, and pass the bottle back and forth, and smoke our weed."

"The Easiest Job in the World"

Tyrone had been in the gang two years when he was allowed to work in the dope house himself.

"The guy who owned it was called 'D'—he was like the top guy in our gang. That's all we called him; I don't know any more of his name. Man, D got rich! He got the dope [crack] from a big-time Colombian guy. The Colombian would sell him kilos. D had a bunch of houses—ours wasn't the only one. And he'd give us like a thousand dollars' or more worth of dope each day to sell. That wasn't hard at all—we could easily sell that much.

"We usually work in pairs. So me and one other dude, we just sit around inside the dope house and wait for customers. No standing out on the street corner, or going to school, or nothing like that. It was the easiest job in the world."

He and his partner would stay for a day or two at a time, he explains.

"One of us would make a run to McDonald's, or we'd go to the store and get stuff for sandwiches," he says. "We'd just bring the food back. We'd also have friends who'd come and visit us—just like when we were younger, you know, they'd bring their weed or their drinks, and we'd get high with them.

"We didn't worry about no cops, no. See, we knew the neighborhood real good. We knew who'd be coming to the door—it was like regular customers. And we had peepholes, so we could see what was going on—if people are getting out of cars, or walking up to the house, or going around to the back door. One of us sort of keeps an eye on each door.

"They don't come inside, either. They just knock. They tell us through the door what they want, like if they want a dime bag or something like that. A dime bag is ten dollars' worth. Then they slide the money under the door, and after we make sure it's the

Two years after joining the Gangster Disciples, Tyrone started selling crack out of a dope house. The extra money allowed him to buy plenty of marijuana, fueling his growing addiction.

right amount, we slide the drugs back out to them. Me and whoever's working with me, we keep three hundred of every thousand dollars we sell."

BEING ADDICTED

Tyrone believes he was addicted to marijuana by the time he was twelve years old.

"I kept smoking, after that first time, because everybody'd tell me how great it was. They told me it was important to know *how* to smoke weed, too. Like, I had to understand how to control it, not let the weed control me. That was good advice, because I really got to like it.

"After a while, it was hard to think about *not* smoking it, you know? It was a habit for me. I don't know back then what would have happened if I'd try to stop. But I sure didn't try."

He smiles. "I was smoking so much back then, because I had so much money. I mean, I was making hundreds of dollars each day selling crack—what was I going to do with it? I bought some clothes—like I told you before, my mom was being a dope fiend, smoking up our family money, so they weren't buying me or Clifton no clothes. And I'd buy food. And shoes. And lots and lots of weed!

"I know that some people say that weed isn't addictive, but that isn't right. I don't know if it's addictive in the same way as crack or heroin or something like that is. Probably not the same. But it's addictive. You get addicted to the way you feel when you are smoking it. You start needing more and more of it, too, to get the same high that you want.

"There was a time, back in Milwaukee, that I was super addicted. I mean, I was spending $150 at a time, just for weed. That would last me like two or three days. And that's a lot of weed, because in Milwaukee it was really cheap."

"THAT'S WHO I AM"

Tyrone emphatically resists the idea that his addiction is a bad thing. Quite the contrary—he feels that he is a better person when he is high.

"My mind is like, if I see someone with weed, I've got to smoke it. That's it," he says. "I won't go insane if I don't have weed one day—that won't happen. I mean, now I don't have much money, so I don't smoke as often as I'd like. And I'm not beating up people, robbing them to get money for my drugs. Not like no dope fiend, like crackheads or whatever.

"It's just smoking weed is how I live my life. Like some people live their lives in a certain way, you know, like maybe they like to fight, or they like to watch karate movies on TV. Me, I like to smoke weed. That's who I am.

"Now it's been three days since I smoked, and I'm not happy about that. I just got no money, like I said. But I know that the next time I got money in my pocket, I'll be smoking. I'll be waking up smoking."

But why? Doesn't he realize there are more valuable things to do with his money than use drugs?

"It's like when I'm high, I'm best. It's the way I feel the best. I'm on point, I understand things around me, I can do things. I'm better when I'm high. If I'm high at school, I learn better; I'm into it. Really!"

He looks quickly around, back and forth, as though he were a basketball player expecting a pass.

"I'm on point, you know what I'm saying? I maintain, I think. I get quiet, let other people talk, but I'm paying attention, I do everything better. I chill with the weed—that's what I mean about controlling it. I watch everything. I drive better when I'm high—it's just the way I am. And when I ain't high, I'm sluggish.

"It takes like five joints to get me high. I smoke them one right after another. I have one, then fire another up right away. Usually I spend like ten dollars, buy myself four or five joints. The best is a megahigh—that's two blunts. That's money, man, that's the best."

He leans back in his chair, thinking of that feeling.

"Following in My Dad's Footsteps"

His gang life in Milwaukee—as well as the money it generated—did not last. Tyrone was shot while working at the dope house.

"Like I said, following in my dad's footsteps," he says with more than a hint of pride. "I was fourteen, still at the same dope house. I was working with this one friend, and he happened to be dope dating. That's when a girl comes over and—let's see..."

Tyrone struggles, trying to explain delicately.

"She gives you, uh, sexual favors, you know? In exchange for some crack? I said to her, 'How about you do me after you do him?' But she's like, 'No.' So I went out for a bit, take a rock with me and find this one lady who's twenty-five. She has sex with me, and I give her the rock. And I come back to the house, and go inside.

"Right after that, someone knocks on the door. We ain't been looking outside, so we don't know who's there. I'm like 'Who is it?' This voice says, 'Give me two dime bags; put 'em under the door.'" Now I'm thinking, man, that ain't how it works—you got to give me the money before I go shoving bags under the door. So I said, 'Come on, man, slide the money.'"

Tyrone says that the person at the door didn't answer, and that confused him.

"I thought maybe it could be one of my friends, just fooling around," he says. "I said, 'Come on, man, quit playing.' I didn't think there was anything suspicious really. So I opened the door—didn't see nobody. So I started to close the door, and all of a sudden somebody pushes it open. They stick a gun inside, and shot me in my back. The bullet came out here," he points, "in my side. And then they shot at me again."

"High or Not, It Was Scary"

Tyrone says he ran to the bathroom, hoping to get away from the gunmen.

"I couldn't see who it was," he says. "I just went in the bathroom. I could hear them out in the kitchen. They're like, 'Where'd he go?' They came to the bathroom door, and they're pushing on it, trying to get in. They're yelling, 'Let us in, or we're going to kill you.' I figure I'm going to die anyway, so I don't open the door. They're trying to open it, but they can't open it all the way, because I'm lying on the floor in front of it.

"And then there's this gun, just an arm and a gun. And a guy's saying, 'Man, where's your work [drugs] at?' I thought, oh, they're after my drugs, you know. So I told them I dropped it on the kitchen floor, because that's what I did.

"But then one of them goes to look in the kitchen, and he's like, 'No, there ain't nothing on the floor—I think that dude's lying. You should kick his ass,' you know, he was cussing. What had happened was, the guy that was in the house with me had heard the shots and grabbed my dope off the floor, you know? He just left out the window then. So there's no dope, and these guys are getting

Tyrone was shot twice during a robbery at the dope house. The traumatic event forced the fifteen-year-old to spend one week recuperating in a hospital and ultimately resulted in his detainment at a juvenile detention facility.

madder and madder. The one guy with the gun is saying, 'Man, don't make me kill you, because I will.' And I told him, 'Man, I don't know where the drugs is at—ask my partner. All I got is some money, see?'"

Tyrone did have fifty dollars, which he gave them, and they left. Weak from loss of blood, he lay on the bathroom floor, wondering what to do.

"I kept remembering what my daddy always told me," he explains. "He said that when you get shot, don't move around, don't run, and don't panic. If you do, you'll bleed more. So I tried not to panic. I could do that pretty good, because I was high, you know? I'd been smoking weed before this happened, so I was more relaxed. Maybe it even saved my life, who knows? It was pretty scary, though, seeing that blood all over the floor. High or not, it was scary. I kept thinking, man, how could so much blood be coming out of me and I'm still alive?"

To the Hospital and to Juvenile Detention

Tyrone dozed off on the floor until he heard a voice calling him.

"It was my friend—I could hear him," says Tyrone. "He was like, 'Tyrone, where you at?' I told him I was in the bathroom, and that I'd got shot in my side. I forgot about the bullet in my back. That didn't hurt nearly as much as my side did.

"Anyway, my friends came in and grabbed the gun, grabbed all the drugs, so if the cops came, they wouldn't know it was a dope house, you know? They helped me get up, and we went outside, real slow. The cold felt good—it was December 11, I remember that. There was like twenty of my gang outside. They're like 'T-rone, T-rone.' That's what they called me. Anyway, I just lay down out there, waiting for the ambulance. I was thinking, I hope that dude that shot me isn't still around somewhere, ready to come back and kill me."

The ambulance came, and Tyrone spent more than a week recuperating from his gunshot wounds.

"The sheriff told me I couldn't be released until he talked to me," he remembers. "But I wouldn't tell him nothing. I didn't really know who it was that shot me, but I had an idea. And I wanted to deal with it myself. So I figured I'd just be released, and I could go home. Only, that didn't happen."

Tyrone had had some trouble back in middle school, and had been ordered to attend counseling sessions every Wednesday as part of his probation. He is reluctant to explain the circumstances, saying only that it was a stupid mistake on his part.

"But what ended up being more stupid was that I stopped going to counseling," he says. "So there was a warrant out for me, for failing to fulfill my obligations, you know? So when I got shot, my name came up on the computer or whatever, and the sheriff didn't release me after all. I got sent to a detention facility—like a hard-core prison for boys."

OUT AT SEVENTEEN

Tyrone was sentenced to one year at the facility, located west of Milwaukee. He ended up spending two years there.

"I got into some bad business there," he says. "Fighting, stuff like that. But it wasn't a bad place, really."

He laughs. "I didn't really mind being there, because my cousin Kevin was there—you know, Cookie's son? It seemed like it was always me and him, me and him. He wasn't there for the same thing I was—he'd gotten in trouble for robbing people, breaking into their houses, like that kind of trouble.

"You hear about places like Wales—hard-core detention places—as being filled with drugs and stuff, but I didn't use no drugs while I was there. I couldn't—there wasn't any around. People snuck in cigarettes, but no weed, no booze.

"So I got out of there when I was seventeen, and I was *so* glad! I got back on the streets again, in no time. The dope house wasn't there no more—it turned into a different place. But that's normal, man. You don't want to keep no dope house for too long, because some people might get suspicious. Anyway, my gang was all glad to see me. They were my family, same as before. And I was back smoking weed, drinking with my friends. But things changed, and it seemed like a good idea to get out of there."

MOVING AWAY

It wasn't that he couldn't have continued selling crack and hanging around with his old friends, insists Tyrone, because he could have.

"Actually, my one aunt had the idea of moving away from Milwaukee," he explains. "She moved here, and thought it was a better place. More businesses, more jobs, friendlier people. There was less crime, too," he says, the irony of his words apparently lost on him.

"So I came to visit for a week, then went back to Milwaukee. Then I came back for another visit, and I liked it here. So I moved up, stayed with my aunt and her kids. At first that worked out real well. But after a while, she wanted her house to be hers, you know, not having guests living there."

Was it his drug use that his aunt objected to? Tyrone thinks not.

"She knew I was smoking and drinking," he says. "She knew I was doing that back in Milwaukee. Hey, she ain't my mother; I'm grown. If my mama and daddy can't tell me nothing, what makes her think I'll let her tell me things? No, my smoking weed is my business—she just wanted me to find my own place, that was all.

"I mean, part of it was that I lost my job. See, she'd gotten me a job at this one nursing home she works at. I was in the food service department. But see, I got fired from that, because I was coming in late all the time. It was only my first job, and I was kind of overexcited, you know, being in a new place on my own. I was doing a lot of partying all night, drinking and smoking weed. So it was hard for me to get up at six the next morning.

"It's too bad the job started so early," he complains. "I mean, if it had meant getting up at nine o'clock or something like that, I would probably have done better. But I'd be up till three, and it wasn't realistic for them to expect me to be there by six, you know what I mean? It just wasn't working out for the way I scheduled my time. So that was one of the reasons my aunt wasn't real happy with how things were going on."

Is he working now? Tyrone shakes his head.

"No. I'm looking a little bit. I'm kind of like in transition, you know? So pretty soon, I bet I'll be getting a job. I'll have to, if I want to get a place of my own. I was staying in shelters, and with friends after I left my aunt's place. And that's hard to hold a job when you're doing that.

"Plus, if I need a job, I can always get a job like the one I had. That don't take no special skill. It's just that kind of job isn't the one I need. I'd like to do something that takes more skill, you know? More kind of aptitude than working in some old people's home."

A Typical Day

His life now is not what he wants. Tyrone has little money. He lives on free meals from youth agencies and continues to stay in shelters or couch-hop for a few nights with friends.

"At the shelter, a typical day is pretty boring," he says. "I'm out of there by nine, and I'd rather sleep. They give you bus tokens, and then I go out, see people. If I'm staying with friends, then I sleep till maybe three in the afternoon, so I can be partying.

"Sometimes I make a little money cleaning up the drop-in center—maybe cleaning the day room, doing some vacuuming, whatever. Just ten dollars or something. But then I can get weed, some Hennessy, some wine, whatever. And cigarettes.

"The way I like to wake up is, first thing I wake up and fire up a cigarette. Then I get out a blunt, and smoke half of it. That boosts my spirit, gets me going. I smoke half of that, then my high goes

Tyrone cleans at a drop-in center for urban youth in order to earn much-needed money. Rather than using his earnings to buy food or shelter, Tyrone maintains his high by purchasing marijuana and alcohol.

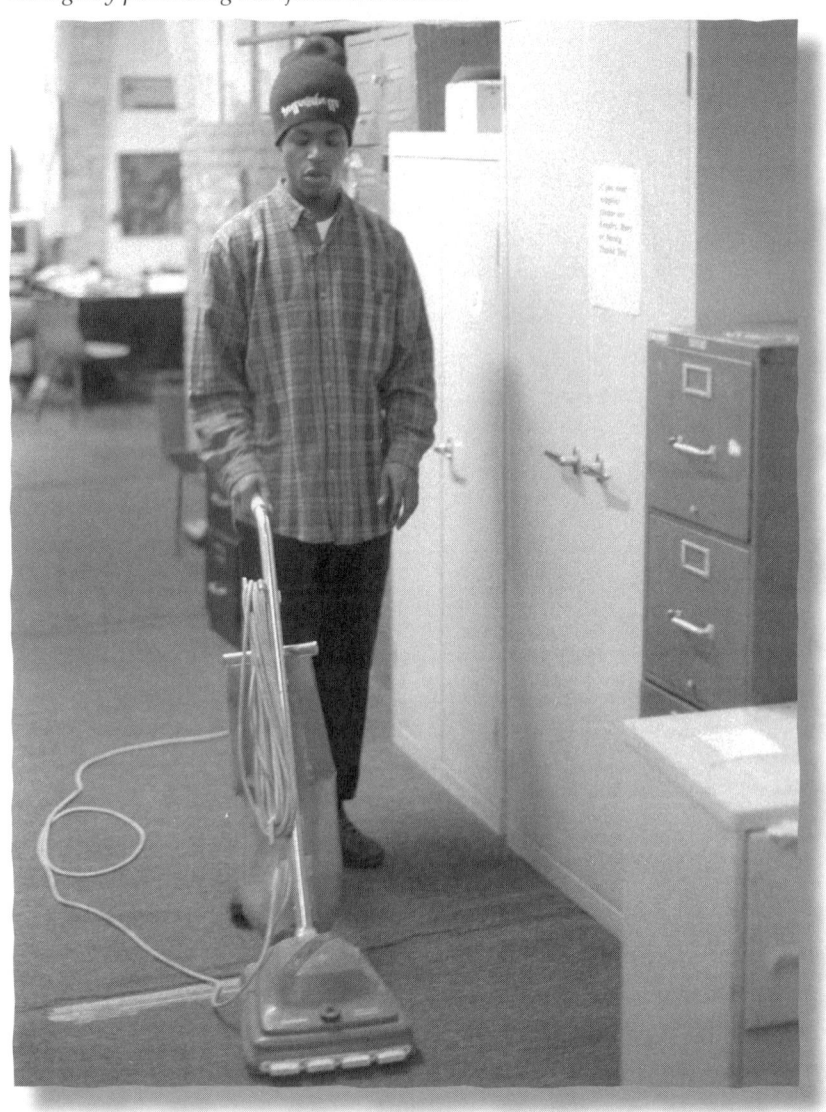

down a little bit, and then I fire it back up, smoke the rest of it. After that I'm hungry, so I go find a meal somewhere, somewhere they're serving free food to kids on the street. You gotta know where to go."

Does he smoke marijuana at any of the shelters or drop-in centers he visits?

"No way," he says emphatically. "That wouldn't be right at all. See, they're trying to help you out, so you can't be doing that stuff right there. That's like, disrespectful. So no, you just wait and do your weed somewhere else."

"IT AIN'T COMPLICATED"

After a few hours, Tyrone says, he sets off downtown, looking for someone with more money than he has.

"I try to find someone to get high with," he says. "I know lots of people that are ready to share what they got. Plus, the dealers know me, too. Sometime I can get with a dealer and work something out. And it's easy to find a dealer!

"I know most of them around Seventh Street. There's a lot that hang out there. And if I was new in town, I'd just look for people my own age. That way, you know they ain't cops. You maybe just say, 'Hey,' and you kind of hold your fingers up like this, like pretending you smoking weed. They'll tell you, 'Man, maybe I got some.' Or if they don't sell, they for sure know who *is* selling.

"It can be boys, girls, don't matter. You just say, 'Man, you got some killer?' That's what you call weed on the streets, sometimes—'killer.' I give them the money all folded up, in my palm, you see?"

He demonstrates, and shrugs. "See, it ain't complicated. He or she just gives you the dope in a little bag. And it goes fast, the whole thing. Takes a couple seconds. It ain't a secret, I'm telling you. Just walk around, look at the kids. They all know who's selling the killer. Just like that."

"I HATE DAYS WHERE THERE'S NO PLAN"

Tyrone is not sure what he will be doing in a month, let alone a year. He smiles good-naturedly and shakes his head when asked about the future.

"I don't want to be married, I know that," he smiles. "I like the ladies, but I don't want to be tied into a relationship like that. I'd like to finish school, then maybe go to college somewhere. I don't know what kind of job I'd get. I'd kind of like to be one of those people—what do you call them? That work with kids? I don't know what they're called. Maybe a counselor, but that isn't it. I don't know.

"I don't want each day to be a struggle, like it is now. I don't want to be unstable financially. I want to get up in the morning and say, 'I have to do this or that.' Like, it's planned out already. That would be good. I hate days where there's no plan. Just lots of time—that's hard."

But does he really think he can continue smoking marijuana? Tyrone looks puzzled.

"Why not?" he asks, frowning. "I don't think I'd ever stop. I don't think I'll always be high, every day, no. Not like if I'm a counselor or whatever, and I'm talking to kids. I wouldn't be high then. I'd try to help them. But if the idea is to always be in control, to be on point, then—I don't know—I can't imagine not smoking."

"My Family's Really Messed Up with Crack"

"But smoking doesn't mean you're high every minute. I can control it—I'm addicted, but I'm in control. I'm a lot different than my family, I'll tell you that. I'm not that kind of addicted. I went back there, you know, about two months ago, just to visit. They're pretty much homeless now. They keep smoking up the welfare money, so they ain't got nothing. My mom is staying with my cousin, my father is living with his mother temporarily. Clifton—he's with my dad sometimes, and sometimes he's with his own friends, too.

"My family's really messed up with crack—and not just my immediate family, either. Like my mom's got six sisters and three brothers, and of all of them only the two youngest boys are okay. The rest are dope fiends, all into crack. They've been doing it so long, I don't think they remember when they *weren't* doing it. It seems like nothing ever changes in our family, except for the worse."

Tyrone has to accept some blame for that, however, because he admits that at one time he was selling crack to his mother and father.

"Yeah, I was selling to them," he says, somewhat defensively. "But that's *their* problem, the way I look at it. See, they got to get over doing crack. At first, I'll admit, I didn't want to sell to them.

Although Tyrone's family continues in a downward spiral of drug addiction, he says he would like to improve his life by finishing school and securing a career; yet he cannot imagine his life without marijuana.

But then I'd think, man, they are going to get it from *somebody*. If it ain't me, it will be somebody else. And what if someone else rips them off, gives them some fake stuff. Or what if they get killed somehow, dealing with some guy who's crazy?

"I'll tell you what I would not do—that's get my brother some crack. He don't do that shit. I would give him some weed, though. I mean, I *have* already done that. I taught him how to smoke it, how to control it, back when he was ten or eleven. And I'd rather have him doing it around me. He's better off."

Teshinda

"IT GOT TO THE POINT WHERE . . . BEING HIGH WAS EVERYTHING TO ME, EVERYTHING THAT MATTERED. IT MADE ME FEEL LIKE I FIT IN . . . I WAS CALM, RELAXED. I FELT LIKE I COULD ALWAYS SAY THE RIGHT THING, OR BE SILENT WHEN THAT WAS COOL, TOO. I WAS A DIFFERENT PERSON."

Author's Note: Teshinda, seventeen, is an African American teen with a long history of being "in the system." Taken from her home when she reported her mother's boyfriend's abuse, Teshinda has been in a long series of foster homes, treatment centers, and shelters. She is a devout believer in the idea that if you're not ready to be helped, you'll never get better. Teshinda is a good example of someone who could have fallen through the cracks, but by her own strength, caught herself in time. She prides herself on having been clean and sober for more than a year.

"I'm so sorry I'm late," gasps the black teen, out of breath from dashing up the steep stairway of the gay and lesbian youth center. "My bus was late, and that's how I get around. I'm Teshinda."

She is heavyset, with short hair and a warm smile. She's wearing jeans and a purple sweatshirt, and is carrying a backpack crammed with notebooks, textbooks, calendars, and pencils. Teshinda sets the backpack on a nearby chair and motions to a scarred wooden table in the conference room.

"I guess this is a good place to talk, huh?" she says, flashing another smile. "I work here, so no one's going to kick us out.

We won't be interrupted, so's you can hear all about what it's like to be a teenage drug addict."

"Mom Wasn't Mean . . . She Was Just Overwhelmed"

Teshinda explains that she is originally from the South Side of Chicago, and has very happy memories of childhood.

"Maybe lots of drug addicts have miserable childhoods," she says. "Mine got miserable later on, that's true. But I'll tell you, I have nothing but happy memories of when I was real young—so maybe I'm not typical.

"I'm sort of the middle child. I've got an older brother, Terrence, an older sister, Taronda, and a little sister, Tekela. Our mom had us when she was really, really young. I'm talking twelve years old, with Terrence. Actually, she had my brother ten days after she turned thirteen. If you saw a picture of her and my brother, she'd look to you like she was almost too young to be baby-sitting, let alone mothering! And my dad wasn't in the picture at all. We don't know him at all."

Teshinda and her siblings lived with their grandmother most of the time. The responsibility of raising four children on her own was too much for her mother, Teshinda says, who was not emotionally equipped to handle a family at such a young age.

"Mom wasn't mean, really," she explains, choosing her words carefully. "She was just overwhelmed. I mean, she had had four kids by the time she was nineteen, and we kind of all grew up together. She tried for a while, I guess—living with us when we were all little. But mostly we were with my grandma.

"I loved living with her, too. She raised us, took care of us. Taught us manners, kept us fed and dressed right. And she worked full-time, too! She had a good job downtown at the Chicago Mercantile Exchange. Sometimes after school, us kids would ride over there on the bus if we didn't feel like going home. It was exciting, visiting her at work. Then we'd all ride the bus home together, with Grandma."

A Lot of Milk

The family moved to Minnesota when Teshinda was five; her aunt had moved first, and decided that the quality of life was better than in Chicago. Teshinda's mother followed soon afterward, and enrolled her children in new schools.

"Even then, away from my grandma, things were fine," Teshinda says. "We had a little apartment, and my mom worked a little. I'm not sure what job she had, but she did work. Anyway, I loved school, loved learning things. And I have pretty good memories about when we were first there. Like the milk money—oh, the milk money!"

Teshinda throws her head back and laughs, remembering.

"I was five, a kindergartener at the time. I remember it was one morning, I told my mom I needed milk money for school. She told me okay, that I should go to her purse and get out a dollar. That

Teshinda listens to headphones while riding on the bus. She now lives in Minnesota, but she recalls happy childhood memories of living in Chicago with her mother, siblings, and grandmother.

would do me for the week, she said. So I did what she said—I pulled out a dollar and put it in my pocket—at least I thought that's what I did.

"What I'd done, evidently, was to pull out a one-hundred-dollar bill, instead. What did I know? I took it to school on the bus and marched up to the teacher's desk and gave it to her. I was proud that I'd remembered, you know how you are when you're five? Anyway, the teacher was like, 'How did you get this?' I told her, 'My mom said it was for my milk for the week.'

"Well, I don't think she exactly believed me! She explained that it wasn't a dollar bill I'd brought. She told me I should take it home, and to be real careful. At the end of the day, she pinned it on my shirt, and buttoned up my jacket over it, so it wouldn't get lost. So I went home, and before I could give it back to my mom, she started telling us how worried she was, how she'd lost money and didn't have enough to pay the bills.

"I'd been planning on sneaking it back into her purse, because I didn't have enough nerve to explain the stupid thing I'd done. I didn't exactly know how she'd react. But she found out soon enough—the teacher called her. I guess that was smart of her, but then everybody knew I didn't know the difference between a one-dollar bill and a hundred!"

"He Caused a Lot of Problems for Our Family"

The children missed their grandmother back in Chicago, but they did all right, Teshinda says. At least, until her mother got a boyfriend. After that, things went downhill pretty fast.

"His name was Donald," she says, her voice a bit unsteady. "And he lived with us; that's the point when my life took a bad turn."

She stops, apparently losing her train of thought.

"Actually, I thank God that I'm even alive today," she says slowly. "See, Donald was an abuser—very much so. The abuse was towards us and towards my mom. There was one time he split my mom's hand, she had to get stitches. He'd taken a sharp knife and cut her with it. He gave her black eyes, split lips.

"It was all temper with him. I mean, he drank and used drugs, but when he was sober, that's when he'd do these things. So you can't blame substance abuse for this stuff. Unfortunately, Donald stayed around for a long time—much, much too long. He caused a lot of problems for our family. More than you'll ever know, really."

Keeping It to Herself

It was, Teshinda says vehemently, a very hard way to grow up. Seeing their mother crying and hurt at the hand of her boyfriend made them all anxious and worried.

"I'd come home and she'd be sobbing over something he'd done to her, or something he'd said," she explains. "But it wasn't just my mom that got hurt. He messed with Terrence, choked him a couple of times. He didn't mess with my younger sister, because she's the baby, you know? He wouldn't have dared do anything to her.

"He tried to touch my older sister, but she didn't let anything happen. She knew better, I guess. But it was different with me. I was younger, and when it all started, I didn't know any better. See, what he did with me was to molest me. He raped me, did things to me—for seven years it went on. It really tore up my family.

"I told my mom about it, yeah, because it felt wrong. I told her a couple of times, hoping she'd do something. But she didn't believe me. That's what she said, anyway. She'd say, 'Oh, you know he wouldn't do anything like that.' So I kept it to myself. I didn't tell anybody. I just told myself, 'That's just how things are.'"

Teshinda says it all went on in her home.

"Like, we'd be watching a movie on TV," she says. "And I'd fall asleep before it was over. And then he'd be the one to volunteer to take me to my room. He'd stay in there, yeah, and things would happen. I was six when it all started."

In and Out of Jail

During this same period, Teshinda says that her mother was spending time in jail—which was almost a relief for the children, for then Donald would be gone, too.

"My mom would get arrested for different things," she says. "She would have drugs, and get caught for possession. She didn't use them, but she was codependent to a drug user, so she was helping Donald. She carried his drugs, bought them for him, whatever. It was marijuana sometimes, crack other times.

"Other times my mom would get caught stealing—shoplifting mostly. She did that a lot, but she must not have been very good at it, because she sure got caught. She'd go into a nice department store and steal clothes. Then she'd bring them back later to get the refund. But over and over, she'd get sent to jail. Usually she'd be gone six months or less."

When her mother was gone, Teshinda says, her family seemed to function pretty well.

"My younger sister didn't do much, because she was pretty little," Teshinda smiles. "But Taronda made sure we were all doing our homework just right. I was the one who talked to everybody else, making sure everybody in the family was happy. I think that's always my role. I like to know how everyone is feeling. My aunt would help out, too.

"But of all of us, Terrence was the best. He was like the father, the brother, the friend to us all. We all knew things would be okay if Terrence said they would. He'd do everything around the house—even make us after-school snacks!"

Teshinda's family life began to deteriorate when her mother's violent boyfriend, Donald, moved in and started subjecting them all to his abuse.

Teshinda laughs. "There was one time we came home and he'd set out glasses of milk and graham crackers with cinnamon on them. We didn't know they came like that at the store—we thought he'd made up this special treat. We spent all this time complimenting Terrence, telling him what a great cook he was. And he had the nerve to accept our compliments, saying 'You're welcome,' to us! Then that night, we were taking out the trash, and there on the top was this box that said Cinnamon Grahams. We really kidded him about that! It sort of became a family joke after that, Terrence's great cinnamon graham recipe. Anyhow, I guess you could say that we did have some good times in all this bad stuff that was going on."

"Please Don't Let It Be at My House"

In one incident, Donald and her mother were both arrested, in addition to one of her aunts and a cousin who'd been staying with them.

"It was because of drugs," says Teshinda. "I remember getting off the school bus, walking home to my apartment with my friend. We were about a block away, and we could see lots of police cars, with their lights flashing and everything. I said to myself, 'Please don't let it be at my house, please don't let it be at my house.' But it was.

"They had the whole apartment complex surrounded, and everybody was outside watching. Our front door was busted in; the cops did that. I was embarrassed and ashamed. And the policemen called my grandma in Chicago, told her that she had to take us. If she didn't, they said, we'd get put in foster homes within seventy-two hours. So we went to live with her until my mom got out of jail.

"There were other times we moved, too. Like one time, my mom decided she needed a break, I guess. She wanted to move to North Carolina. See, my aunt moved there—she was the one who'd moved to Minnesota before. Well, my mom followed, along with me and my little sister. My older sister wanted to stay in Chicago with my grandma, and Terrence got sent down to Texas to live with my uncle for a while. I didn't like that our family was split up, because we'd been close, you know? And I didn't want that to stop. But I was only eight then, so I didn't have much say in the matter. I guess you could say that my life kind of got stirred up in the mix."

WITHOUT TELLING ANYONE

Her mother's interest in living in North Carolina didn't last long, however. Without telling anyone, she went back to Minnesota, leaving Teshinda and her younger sister alone.

"It was one of the scariest times of my life," Teshinda admits. "Things had been okay. I'd been lonesome for Terrence and everything, but my mom had a job working at my school down there and things were okay. But one day, my aunt was at our house, and found my mom's suitcases all packed in the closet. I remember that real well.

"My aunt asked my mom what all that was about, but my mom denied she was planning to go anyplace. I just forgot about it. But then, the next day, she left me and Tekela alone in the house and went out. We didn't know where she was—I just expected her to come home any minute. But the hours went by, and nothing happened. Me and Tekela were crying. We were both real scared. You know how you start crying so hard, you get all stuffed up in your nose, you can't breathe? That's how it was for us.

"The phone rang a couple of times, but we couldn't reach it. We just sat on the couch, looking out the window for my mom screaming and crying because we were scared. We didn't even turn on the lights when it got dark. The next day my aunt came over, looking for my mom. She says, 'Where is she?' I told her, 'She left yesterday.' Boy, my aunt was mad!"

Teshinda's aunt sent the two little girls back to Chicago to live with their grandmother again. And when, weeks later, their mother came to Chicago to claim her daughters, she was punished for her irresponsibility.

"My grandma's motto was always: 'Your kids should always be with you,'" explains Teshinda. "It didn't matter what the reason was that my mom left—it was wrong, in my grandma's eyes. And when my mom came to get us, my grandma wouldn't let us go. She was so mad at my mom, accused her of abandoning her children, which I guess she did.

"That was a real frightening evening, too, because my oldest uncle punished my mom for that. Right there, he gave her a whupping—no spanking, 'cause in our family you didn't get spankings. He hit her with a broomstick. I remember thinking, man, she's a grownup but she's *still* getting a whupping! Me and my sister, we watched the whole thing while we were sitting in the dining room. My mom had blood all over her, and she was crying.

"When the whole thing was over, my grandma let my mom take us. It was like, she got her punishment, and now everything's okay. I wish we hadn't gone back, though, because Donald was back there, too. And the sexual abuse started right up when we got back to Minnesota."

Over and Over

Did she ever think of telling her grandmother or Terrence about what Donald was doing? Teshinda says no.

"I maybe thought about it," she says. "I wondered sometimes if he was doing the same thing to my sisters or to Terrence. I think I didn't tell my grandma because I was ashamed. I don't know—I

After suffering through years of sexual abuse, Teshinda finally found the courage to speak out; as a result, she was placed in a foster home.

wanted to just stay away from him, and have the whole thing be solved that way. I'd try to avoid him, but you know, when you're a little kid, you have to be home at night.

"Just the thought of being home alone with him was scary. I can remember one time I'd gone to the bus stop, when I remembered I'd forgotten my homework back on the kitchen table. I didn't want to go to school without it, because I was a good student, and I liked my teacher. But boy, I really didn't want to go back there. What if I missed my bus, and I had to stay home all day with him. Well, that's what happened. I thought I could outrun the bus, get home and get back to the bus stop. But I wasn't fast enough, and I had to stay home.

"He told me sometimes that if I thought about telling anyone, I should think twice. He said he'd hurt my mom if I told. I believed him, too. See, I was really protective of my mom back then. I didn't want her to suffer more than she was already, you know?

"I used to have nightmares, though. I'd wake up and couldn't get back to sleep. My heart was just banging away in my chest. I was afraid to go to the bathroom, too. I thought maybe he'd be behind the door, waiting to get me.

"I think back on that now, and I wonder more than ever why my mom put up with that. Once she was going to leave him; she'd had enough, she said. That's when he cut her, when she threatened to leave. When he did that, all us kids started crying, and he left. She called the cops that time, and they took him to jail. But then she wouldn't press charges! One day, maybe two—after that he'd come right back."

TELLING

Teshinda finally told her secret when she was in fifth grade.

"I'd had enough, I guess," she shrugs. "What happened was, in school we were in health class. You know how you get to talking about different situations? Well, that day, I'd come to school crying, because Donald had raped me the night before. And I just told. I told my teacher. The words just came out.

"She called down the social worker at school, and I told her, too. Well, I didn't go home that night. A policeman came to the school, and took me to the hospital for a checkup. He was really nice, took me out to eat and everything. And from the hospital I went to a foster home. It just happened—just like that."

Teshinda says that her mother refused to accept the truth of Donald's abuse, and refused to press charges.

"Even so, my sisters got taken out of there the next month," she says. "And it was okay at first. Maybe it sounds as if it should have been more—I don't know—traumatic? But it wasn't. My mom wasn't home a lot of the time anyway, and I sure didn't miss Donald. It might have been a positive thing, us being out of that house, except for the way I was acting."

"I Wasn't a Nice Person Then"

Teshinda says that she was a very angry girl in that foster home, and she looks back on that time with shame.

"I was mean," she says in a small voice. "I had lots of anger in me—from the abuse, from the way our family was. But that's not an excuse; it's just the way I was. I mean, today I think of myself as a sweet person, someone who is kind. But I wasn't a nice person then.

"The lady we lived with wasn't as loving to me or my two sisters as she was to her other kids. She'd adopted them, and you could tell she favored them over us. I guess that would be normal. But all I knew is that it gave me an excuse to be mean, to be angry.

"I took it out on my sisters. I fought with them, said mean things to them. And to be fair, I remember them saying some mean things back to me. Like, for instance, I knew they blamed me for telling about what Donald did, and destroying the family. They saw it that way, that I was responsible for the family falling apart. And maybe part of me believed them. Like I said before, when you're young—fifth grade—what do you really know?"

"It Was an Awful Thing to Do"

Teshinda's temper got her thrown out of that foster home, she admits.

"I pulled a knife on one of my sisters," she says. "I take the blame; it was an awful thing to do. The family called the police, but I ran before they arrived. They caught up with me, though, and took me to a juvenile detention center. From there I went to another place. The next seven years would be a string of detention centers, foster homes—I counted sixty-five of them all together. I never stayed anyplace for too long. Actually, eight months was the longest.

"It was always kind of hard going to a new place; you never knew if they were going to accept you or not, or how they'd act toward you. I pretended not to worry about it, but I really did. Anyway, this second place was pretty nice. I screwed it up, though.

"I started stealing a lot," Teshinda says quietly. "I'd steal from kids at school—I took stuff out of their backpacks when no one was around. I'd even steal from teachers, from their desk drawers. The best time for that was when we were planning to go on a field trip or something like that. I'd wait until the teacher left the room, and I'd go in her drawer and get the money, the cash parents would send with their permission slips, you know?"

Teshinda says that she also stole from her foster family, and when the news of the thefts at school surfaced, the adults figured out that she was stealing there, too.

"They wouldn't let me go back to that school," she explains, "so I got put in an alternative school, one for kids with problems. I still stayed with that same foster family, but a new school. That time was a turning point for me, a real bad one."

Fitting In

She'd always had a problem fitting in, Teshinda says, but never as much as at that school.

"I was a real misfit," she admits. "And I'll tell you, it wasn't new for me. I'd been teased for being heavy, because I was smart in school, whatever. But here it was bad. I got teased a lot because of my name—it was too ghetto. 'Teshinda' means a kind of African drum. I like my name, but the kids really got on me because of that."

She sighs. "You know, it's hard to figure out. Some kids don't act like they care one way or another if they fit in, but they do anyway. I cared a lot, but I never could. Why could some kids do it and not me? I didn't have a clue. I was always too something, I guess. But at this school, at that time of my life, I decided I was going to fit in whatever it took."

What it took, she says, was a lot of new experiences.

"I started using drugs," Teshinda says. "I started hanging out with a lot of gang kids—ones I'd never really hung out with before. They were Crips, most of them. I was smoking weed, drinking beer. I didn't mind the weed so much, but I'll tell you, I hated the taste of beer. But those kids were like, 'Come on,

Teshinda's temper and reckless behavior got her thrown out of a string of foster homes and placed in detention centers. She was unable to rehabilitate herself and finally became involved with a gang.

you're almost thirteen!' So I stayed with it, and from there, graduated to hard liquor—tequila, gin and juice, whatever.

"Most of those kids were older, and they had ways of getting drugs and liquor that I didn't. We'd drive around—there was always someone who had a car—and just generally got into trouble. If I needed to chip in money, I'd steal. That wasn't anything new to me, like I said before."

Addicted

It didn't take Teshinda long to realize that she had gone from being a casual user of marijuana to an addict. And to anyone who claims that marijuana isn't addictive, Teshinda strongly objects.

"Right—it's not addictive," she snorts. "Yeah, sure. Don't tell me that—I know better. It got to where that's all I was doing, was smoking weed. I'd do it with my friends sometimes, but usually I used it by myself. And I used it constantly.

"It got to the point where weed, being high, was everything to me, everything that mattered. It made me feel like I fit in, in ways I'd never felt before. I was calm, relaxed. I felt like I could always say the right thing, or be silent when that was cool, too. I was a different person. I wasn't the girl who'd been abused. I was better—I was popular—I was at peace.

"When I sobered up, of course, things were still the same as they'd always been," she says sadly. "The bad life was still there. I was still in a foster home, my family still was mad at me, I was still overweight. So, yeah, it was just a temporary solution. But it was addictive! I couldn't stop, didn't want to stop."

Therapy

During this time, Teshinda was seeing a therapist, by the terms of the court order that had placed her and her sisters in foster homes.

"My therapist's name was Cheryl," she says, smiling. "I saw her for seven years—I still see her now and then. She and my case aid were the only two adults who were constant in my life, from the minute I got put in foster care until now.

"In a lot of ways, their just being there for me was a real positive influence, really an important part of my life. Although—I got to be honest," she says, rolling her eyes. "I wasn't exactly open with Cheryl at first. The whole first year I saw her, I never said a word. I didn't talk at all. She'd pick me up, take me for ice cream or whatever, and I'd just sit there. She was really patient.

"But about the time I was having trouble in this alternative school, that's when I started up talking to Cheryl. I don't remember what it was exactly—I was mad at my foster mom because she wasn't letting me go out to my friend's house or something like that. So I started telling Cheryl how mad I was, how angry. Other than that, I really didn't know what she expected me to talk about with her. I mean, she knew about the abuse I'd gone through. That was the reason for the therapy in the first place.

"But she didn't know about my drug abuse, or at least the extent of it. She suspected it, I know. See, she knew I was getting more and more into the gang. I mean, I was walking around with my blue rag hanging out of my pocket—it was hard to miss! And she was getting reports from school, how I was getting in trouble for things at school. I'd been caught coming in to school high, and once I got suspended for having liquor on the premises. But she didn't know how much I was using. At that time I was just at the point where I didn't care about much of anything. And that feeling lasted a long, long time."

Lady T

As a Crip, Teshinda had a gang name—Lady T.

"Sometimes it was 'Mama T,'" she says, "because I sort of took care of everybody. I was the one everyone could talk to. That was sort of my role, all through my life, even back with my family.

"You wouldn't have known me back then—you wouldn't have believed how different I was. I was a fighter. I was down for myself, down for whoever I was with. Whatever was called for, I did. And I had a bad attitude. You could be a stranger walking by me, and if you looked at me funny, I was ready to fight you.

"I usually hung with the boys in the gang. I was always a tomboy, you know? So that was more comfortable for me, but I did get along with some of the girls. In a gang, you usually have to get jumped in, you know, but because there were some of my cousins who'd been Crips, I got blessed in—that way I didn't have to fight or anything like that.

"So I got blessed in by the girls, but they turned out to be too weak for me. So I chose to get jumped in by the boys, and I did it okay. Then later, I wanted to get higher up in the ranks, so I had to sleep with some people who were higher up than me."

How old was she, when this was going on? Teshinda thinks a minute.

"Thirteen, I guess," she says.

Wake and Bake

Her drug use increased at this time, too. Every day became a blur of marijuana and liquor, and though she was occasionally caught and suspended from school, she continued to use drugs.

As Teshinda became increasingly involved in her gang, she also became increasingly addicted to marijuana. She now meets with counselors at a treatment center in an effort to keep her addiction and anger things of the past.

"It was basically 'wake and bake'—plain and simple," she says. "You wake up, get high right away, and stay high all day. You have a joint in the morning, go to school high. Then you go to the bathroom with your friends and get high again.

"We didn't drink as much as we smoked weed, but sometimes we brought water bottles that weren't really water, you know? Anyway, after school we'd get high again, and go home that way. Smoke some in the evening, go to sleep that way. Really, the only time I wasn't high was when I was sleeping."

Eventually, the foster family who had stood by her for eight months had had enough, and Teshinda still regrets that she let them down.

"I feel bad," she says. "My foster mother had seen me over and over coming in high, or drunk, or both. And she tried to be patient, tried to be supportive. But at some point, she just had to say 'Enough.' So that's what happened.

"I went to a treatment center, where the staff tried to deal with the cause of all the anger I had—and I had plenty of anger. I was depressed, I was bulimic—at that point I'd been trying to get thin by making myself throw up all the time. Another way of trying to fit in. So they dealt with the eating disorder, too."

SUICIDAL

However, the treatment she received at that point was ineffective. Her drug use not only continued—it increased and expanded.

"It wasn't only weed," she says. "Actually at this time, I really got into inhalants. Bleach, fingernail polish, furniture polish, glue, the stuff to spray to make your house smell good—it didn't seem to matter. Inhalants, I have to say, became my drug of choice. They were better than a joint, 'cause they were quicker.

"But at this same time, I was getting really suicidal. It was partly the drugs, yeah. I mean, I wasn't dealing with anything in my life then. It was all about escaping, about getting high and forgetting about things. But I was angry, and I really didn't like myself.

"You could tell that by how I was treating myself—my body. I was so self-destructive. Sometimes it was overdosing—I did that a few times. I used Tylenol 3; I'd been given that for some bad headaches I'd been having. And I'd mutilate myself, burn myself with matches or lighters, or maybe cut myself up. What I did a lot was use erasers on my skin. See here?"

She rolls her sleeves up and shows long scars on her arms.

"This is from me trying to erase myself. I did it so hard, so deep, it made permanent marks. I did this stuff at different foster homes sometimes, but usually it was at shelters. It seemed like there was less structure there, and for me, having lots of time on my hands was just what I didn't need. That's when I started feeling the worst. If I was busy, I didn't have those feelings as often. But as soon as I was off on my own—and I was a big-time loner most of the time—I was depressed again."

Outsmarting the System

Because she had attempted suicide, Teshinda had to submit to routine UA, or urinalysis, tests. After one of the tests showed drugs in her system, she was sent to a drug treatment center.

"You weren't supposed to use anything at this place," she says. "They supposedly have a good reputation, helping kids get off their substance abuse problems. But even though we didn't have access to any weed or anything like that, I continued to use.

"See, they left the door to the cleaning closet unlocked," she says with a wry smile. "There were all kinds of janitorial supplies in there, stuff I could inhale. So on the way back to the showers or something, I'd sneak in there and take something. I'd be huffing in the shower, or maybe in my room.

"The funny thing was, all the time I was there, the staff thinks I'm doing great. I'm even getting rewards for being clean and sober. You get medallions, you know, for reaching certain points, and I got my six-month medallion. They didn't even know that right under their noses, I'm getting high all the time. Everybody was making such a big deal about me, telling me how proud they were of me. Even Cheryl—I was lying to her, too."

Did she feel a little guilty, accepting praise for something she hadn't done? She frowns.

"Not at all. I didn't feel bad," she explains. "I was protecting myself, doing what I always did."

Getting Caught

Because she was thought to be doing well in her battle against drug use, Teshinda was placed in a foster home. She worked two jobs, as well as attending classes at the local high school.

"It was a nice family," she says. "But I messed this place up, too. See, I was due to get my nine-month medallion—completely stupid, since I continued to use drugs and drink. And the day before I was to get it, I went out and really got messed up. I was with friends, yeah. So I came home, drunk and high from smoking weed.

"I got put in a shelter for a while, then went back to that same foster home. They were still willing to have me; I don't really know why. Anyway, I admitted to the people at the shelter as well as to my foster family that I'd been using the whole time. It wasn't just a one-time relapse, like they were thinking.

"I don't think they really knew what to do with me, except they were all willing to give me another chance. I messed this up, too. I got caught at school with an open bottle in my book bag. My teacher saw it, I guess, when I went to pull out a folder for class. Anyway, I'd been caught—again. So just like before, it was back to the shelter. And I knew this time I wouldn't be going to any foster home."

"I Needed a Family"

At the shelter Teshinda's depression became more pronounced, and she tried to kill herself again.

"I slit my wrists—and this time I did it the right way," she says. "You know, there's right and wrong ways to do it. But they found me, took me to the hospital and stitched me up. But I was so sad. See, they can stitch you up, make you stop bleeding. But they couldn't make me feel less sad. I was angry, depressed, didn't care about anything. I knew I would try to kill myself again—it was just a matter of time and opportunity.

"A lot of my sadness was because of my family. I felt like there was no one in my life that loved me, or cared about me. I saw Cheryl once a week, but that wasn't the same. I needed a family, but I sure didn't have one."

Her eyes fill with tears momentarily, and she brushes them away.

"I hadn't seen Terrence or my sisters. I felt like they were mad at me, at least the girls were, because they held me responsible for breaking up our family. Because I told on Donald, everything bad happened. But I felt like, hey, I told on Donald to stop the bad stuff that was happening *to me*."

After her stay in the hospital, she was sent to another treatment facility. Unlike the other ones she had stayed in, this one scared her.

"I was the only black person," she says. "I mean, I didn't let on that I was scared, but I was. I wanted somehow to make an impression on the other people there, so they wouldn't mess with me, you know? So the first day I was there, I took out my Adidas outfit—money green. I knew that would make a statement. My money Adidas, that's what I wore. They'd know I wouldn't take anything from them, I figured."

"I Was Ready to Be Honest"

Teshinda relapsed very soon after arriving at the treatment center. Like the last center she'd been in, this one kept the janitor's closet unlocked, and she began using inhalants.

"It was different here, though," she says. "I can't tell you why, because I don't know. But I admitted what I'd done right away to the director. She didn't catch me—this time *I* was the one who told *her*. I don't know why—maybe I was ready to be honest or something. I told her I'd been huffing, and I even told her about the door being unlocked.

"She got this real funny look on her face, and said, 'Show me.' So I took her over to the door of the cleaning closet, and told her how there was all this stuff in there, but the door was never locked. She got really mad then. Not at me, but at the situation, I guess, because of all those chemical dependency kids there. She figured other kids had been doing it all along, too. I don't know about that, I told her, since I used by myself."

At age seventeen, Teshinda is legally emancipated and steadfastly maintaining her sobriety. The high school senior attends school and works at the espresso bar (pictured) in the local gay and lesbian center.

After her admission to the director, there were some changes, Teshinda says.

"Well, the obvious one is that there was a lock on the door, and a big sign saying THIS DOOR MUST REMAIN LOCKED AT ALL TIMES. That's one thing that happened. But there were some things that started happening with me, too. I started learning to talk about myself. We had these group sessions, where we'd tell about things going on in our lives, or stuff we'd done. And I admitted for the first time that I was an addict, that I was addicted both to drugs and alcohol.

"I learned some things, too—some things that didn't make me feel too good. Like, some of the kids told me that they were really scared of me, that I frightened them. Boy! I told them, 'You guys don't know how that makes me feel—I mean, I scare myself at times. I don't want to be a hardass, I don't mean to scare people away.' But I told them about my life, how I'd had this abuse, and how I'd prostituted myself, and about the drugs, and being gay, and my family, about everything. It just started coming out, you know?

"Some of the people in my group told me that I was brave just to be alive. I didn't think of myself as being brave, really. I told them it was just surviving—nothing more than that. Anyway, I got so much respect when I started sharing stuff like that. I mean, I'd thought that my money Adidas outfit was the key, but it wasn't."

MOVING ON

Teshinda stayed at the treatment facility for four months. During that time she was treated for her depression; she also continued to get counseling.

"Normally the most you can stay there is three months, but I was in and out of the hospital while they figured out my medications for depression, so they gave me four months. And leaving that treatment center was hard. I'd made good friends there—some of the counselors and nurses were almost like family to me. I mean, some were more family than my real family, if you know what I mean.

"One of the things I did before I left was to contact all the foster families I'd lived with over the years. I called them all, told them how sorry I was for the way I'd behaved. They were all nice about it, too. They were very forgiving. I still see one of the families I lived with.

"Anyway, in January 1998, I left after graduating. Graduating means that you have to complete ten of the twelve steps to recovery. I did all twelve, actually. I'd earned the trust of the staff, been allowed to leave the place for activities and things. And I didn't ever betray that trust, not since the first time I relapsed. I was someone they could count on.

"Like, if people came to me or told me secrets—stuff they were doing that was wrong—I was quick to tell the staff. See, to someone who hasn't been through treatment, that may sound like I'm being disloyal. But what I'd be doing if I kept that secret is called 'enabling,' and that's a bad thing to do. It's like I'm supporting their using drugs or drinking, or whatever. I'm hurting them, doing that. There were five rules that could get you kicked out of that place, and enabling was one of them. No way was I about to do anything bad. I was done with that. I wanted to change my life around."

"IF I WAS GOING TO RELAPSE, IT WOULD HAVE BEEN THEN"

Feeling better about herself than she had in many years, Teshinda went from the treatment center to another foster home.

"I was pretty optimistic," she says. "But I'll tell you, something happened that I wasn't expecting. I got kicked out of that foster home, and it wasn't for relapsing, because I didn't relapse. What they kicked me out for was being gay.

"I hadn't told them—it wasn't an issue. But they saw the posters I had up in my room—Ellen, Queen Latifah, [rapper] Queen Pin. A bunch of women who'd come out, you know? So they figured it out, and after that I wasn't welcome. So for the next six months, I had no home. I was kind of back in the system, going from temporary shelter to shelter.

"Yeah, I was depressed then. I thought I was on the right road, you know, and all of a sudden something like that happened. But—I gotta say—I am proud of one thing. I didn't relapse during that time. And if I was going to relapse, it would have been then. That's for sure. But I stayed clean and sober all that time."

Today at seventeen, Teshinda is legally emancipated, meaning that the court has allowed her to have control over her life. Her mother is no longer her legal guardian.

"I'm a senior in high school," she says proudly. "I'm going every day; I have friends among the teachers and the students. I don't

Fully recovered, Teshinda now holds a job, lives on her own, and plans to attend college. She is optimistic about her future and hopes to one day inspire other teens to see their full potential.

see my mother anymore—she's got a new boyfriend who is physically abusive, too. He's as bad if not worse than Donald. But that's what she wants, I guess. I wish things were different, but they're not. She's got to be the one to put a stop to all that.

"I've got my own apartment, through a program that helps teens like me that have been in crisis. And I have a job working here at the center. And things feel pretty good. I'd like to go to college after this year; I think I'd like to be a psychologist. Maybe I'd be a counselor—I don't know for sure. I think about maybe running a foster home for kids someday, too."

She grins wickedly. "I'd like to have them send me the baddest kids around, too. The ones everybody else has given up on, the ones who can't be helped. That one's bad? Yeah, give him to me! See, social workers didn't even want my case, because I was like that. But I'm living proof that people can change, and good things can happen."

Jorge

> "SO I'D GIVEN UP. I'D HIT BOTTOM—I JUST DIDN'T CARE ANYMORE WHAT WAS GOING TO HAPPEN TO ME . . . THEY ALL KNEW I NEEDED HELP. BUT NOT ME. I DIDN'T KNOW IT. OR AT LEAST, I WASN'T ADMITTING IT TO ANYONE, INCLUDING MYSELF."

Author's Note: Jorge, known by many as Ryan, considers himself a former drug user. At nineteen, he has gone through rigorous treatment at a hard-core state center. Addicted to both marijuana and LSD, Jorge is now in transitional housing, waiting for his first apartment. By his own admission, he has made many mistakes, hurting his family most of all.

The day is unusually warm for December, and Jorge's apartment—although amazingly clean for a teenage boy living on his own—is almost stifling.

"I'm going to prop up a window," he says, jamming an empty plastic liter bottle of pop between the sill and the window. "It's not usually so hot in here."

After dialing a series of numbers on his phone, he looks up. "I'm sorry about all this," he says with a smile. "I get lots of phone calls, so I thought it would be better if I just reroute them to my pager. That way we won't keep getting interrupted."

Jorge starts to speak, and then interrupts himself.

"You know," he says, "there's something I've got to make clear. There might be people coming to the door who call me Ryan, you know? Well, that's legally my name—or at least it is for the time being. I'm in the process of getting it changed to Jorge. So I didn't want that to throw you off."

Does changing his Irish-sounding name to an obviously Spanish-sounding one have anything to do with his experiences as a drug addict? He smiles ruefully.

"Yeah," he says. "In a way, it really does."

ABANDONED IN BOGOTÁ

Jorge began his life in Bogotá, Colombia. His mother, whose name is Carma Rose, abandoned him at a hospital when he was a baby.

"Of course, I don't remember anything about that," he says matter-of-factly. "I was only a couple of months old then. But I had gotten polio, and she didn't know how to take care of me."

Polio, he explains, was far more common in Colombia eighteen years ago than here in the United States.

"There was vaccine, sure," he says. "But Colombia has so many poor people, it wasn't real uncommon for people not to get their kids vaccinated. When I got it, I was two months old. My mother brought me into the hospital because I had a real high fever and was crying. She couldn't do anything to make me feel better, I guess.

"She visited me a couple of times, and then stopped coming. The hospital finally figured out what was wrong with me, and treated me as best they could. And after a while, they gave me to an orphanage. The people at the orphanage were trying to place children with American families, so they gave us American names. My mom had named me Jorge, but the orphanage changed it to Ryan."

"THEY WERE GOOD PARENTS"

Jorge was adopted by an American couple when he was eighteen months old.

"Jim and Cheryl," he says. "They adopted me sort of right at the peak of my illness. See, the virus has to kind of run its course, and after that, it's real common to have aftereffects. Like, as you can see, I walk with a pretty severe limp.

"Anyway, I was real sick at first, always in bed. My mom and dad have told me that I couldn't even walk until I was four years old. Up until that point, I'd pull myself along on the ground, because I couldn't even crawl that well. But I was lucky in a couple of ways. One is that I came to the United States. See, if you got polio in Colombia and you were like ten years old, the hospital or orphanage or whatever would just kick you out with a crutch. It's such a poor, poor place, man. It's just amazing how poor that country is. So for me being a little kid with polio, I was pretty lucky to have been put on a plane going to America.

"And they were good parents; that's another reason I was lucky. They gave me all the attention in the world when I was young. They'd do everything for me. And like I said before, I was pretty needy. I had to have four surgeries when I was a kid, just to correct some of the damage from my disease. One operation was on my heel cord here, another one to help me get more mobility in my foot, to move it up and down. When I was in—sixth grade, I think—the doctors drilled two holes in my right leg to slow down the growth so my left leg could catch up. And my mom and dad were real supportive, real caring."

"The Hardest Part of My Whole Life"

Jorge says he was active as a youngster, even with his physical limitations. Even so, he was teased a lot.

"I couldn't walk that great, you know," he says. "I mean, it was obvious that I had problems. But I acted like I didn't have any; I tried to put on a big image, that I was completely fine, completely okay.

"But the kids teased me. When I was in the younger grades, it wasn't such a big deal. Everybody gets teased when they're little—anything that makes you different, whether it's red hair or being fat or skinny, or left-handed, or whatever. I don't remember it bothering me so much then.

"But by fifth and sixth grade, kids were really making fun of my leg. I got called 'gimp,' or 'cripple.' I remember, I used to go home crying. That was like the hardest part of my whole life, I think. I didn't get it, how kids could be that way. I didn't call other kids names, you know, so I thought they'd treat me better. But I just kept being mocked, called 'Limpalong,' whatever. My parents just told me to ignore them, and reassured me that I was okay.

"It was about this time, too, when the whole situation of me being adopted kind of got more real to me. And I won't lie—it made me feel resentful in a lot of ways toward my parents. I felt like they took me away from my biological mother, from the country where I was born. I was Jorge before, and then I became Ryan.

"I had a lot of anger toward them, too. I mean, I can look at that situation now, because I'm nineteen, and I can see that it wasn't Jim and Cheryl who took me away from my mother. I mean, my mother abandoned me. But I was angry just the same. And I'd show it. I'd say things like 'You're not my real mother,' or 'You can't tell me what to do.' I wanted them to stay out of my life."

Although polio has left Jorge with a pronounced limp, it hasn't stopped him from playing basketball on a wheelchair league.

Getting High the First Time

It was at this time in his life when Jorge had his first encounter with drugs.

"I played wheelchair basketball—in fact, I still do," he says with some pride. "I've been playing since I was nine. I don't use a wheelchair any other time except for sports. Anyway, I was eleven, and our team was at a tournament somewhere. We were in this hotel, and one of the kids on my team asked me if I wanted to smoke some weed. I said sure.

"You know," he smiles, "you hear a lot of times how people will say that they had no reaction to pot the first time they tried it, how they didn't get high at all? Well, that wasn't me. I really got high, and I loved it. I thought it was really cool, and all I could think about was, I want to do this again.

"That was the first thing I asked Joe, the kid who smoked with me the first time. I said, 'Can I get some more of that?' But he's like, 'No, you got to buy it.' I asked him how much, and he said he'd bring another joint when we had our next basketball practice. He told me to bring ten dollars."

Jorge laughs. "All I could say was, 'Ten *dollars?*' It seemed like so much money to me. I mean, I mowed our lawn at home every week for twenty dollars, and my parents put the money in the bank for me. But man, I wanted more of that weed so much, I would have found a way to get it, even at twice that price!"

Stealing

Jorge's immediate problem was getting his hands on ten dollars by the following week.

"What I did was, I stole it," he admits. "I was so obsessed about the whole thing, I went in my sister's piggy bank and my mom's purse to scrape ten bucks together. And true to his word, Joe brought the joint to practice.

"I smoked it right away, right out in front of the gym before practice. I'll tell you something else—I had absolutely no idea that it was illegal. I guess I figured it wasn't something my parents would want me doing, just like smoking a cigarette or something. But beyond that, I didn't have a clue. I remember after smoking it, I went in and tried to play basketball. My coach was mad at me because I wasn't doing anything right. He didn't know I was high.

Jorge started smoking marijuana at age eleven and soon became obsessed with getting high. When he had trouble coming up with the money to buy the joints, he admits that he resorted to stealing.

"After that, it was sort of off and on for me. I couldn't really keep the pace up, spending ten dollars for a joint. Plus, when I think about it, Joe was making out pretty good, since he always shared it with me, and I was paying for it. But there was no way I could come up with the money I needed to get high all the time. At one point I was stealing cassette tapes from the store and selling them, just to raise money to buy a joint."

Jorge says he also stole money occasionally from his parents for drugs, and by sixth grade he was stealing from his fellow students.

"I used to volunteer to be the one to bring the lunch money down to the office," he says. "At that point, I was smoking pretty regularly, and buying about forty dollars worth at a time—that's about five big joints. Anyway, I'd get the envelopes that kids had put their lunch money in for the next week, and I'd head downstairs. But I'd go into the bathroom, and sort of go through the envelopes, looking for ones that had cash instead of checks.

"By the time kids were getting charged for lunches their parents had already paid for, it was too late. I mean, it was the past week, or even two weeks, and who remembers the last one to handle that money? Even so, after a while the school stopped letting students take the money down. So I never got caught.

"I was also coming by money honestly; I started mowing two extra lawns each week during the summer, so I'd have another forty dollars. Every bit of that went to buy weed."

Moving

"We moved before seventh grade started. We had lived in the city, but my parents wanted a bigger house. You'd have to call us upper middle class. My parents made plenty of money. My mom is the secretary in a legal firm, and my dad works at the county government center.

"So we moved [to a wealthier suburb] west of the city, to a totally different neighborhood. It was a real culture shock for me, let me tell you. I was like the only Hispanic person out there. In a way I was already sort of confused culturally, being adopted by a white family, you know? And my parents raised both my younger sister and me—she's adopted, from Bogotá, also [but not my biological sister]—to be more white than Hispanic. It was sort of like not fitting in anyplace.

"Anyway, I guess I dealt with that by putting on a big attitude, being the tough guy. A lot of that attitude went right toward my parents. I was mad when I didn't get what I wanted, and I let them know. I felt like they didn't get stuff that I wanted, even though they sure had the money. Like maybe I'd get off-brand shoes instead of the Nikes or Adidas I wanted. Or if I wanted my hair cut a certain way, the answer was no. Even the music I liked—rap—wasn't okay with them. So it wasn't always about money. But sometimes it was.

"If I didn't get what I wanted, I'd steal or get in trouble some other way. I also used to lash out at them. I wasn't open at all with them; I know that now. If they'd try to talk to me, I'd be like, 'Fuck you,' and I'd walk away. I didn't want to deal with them. I'd do a lot of door slamming, punching walls. I started doing a lot of body mutilation—cutting myself when I was mad. I'd also pierce my ears when I was angry—just take an earring and shove it through my earlobe. I didn't care if it hurt. That was the point."

This was also a time when he turned the physical abuse outward, towards his parents.

"I got to the point where I was pushing and hitting my dad," he says, speaking very softly. "I got the police called on me four times for that. I'd get taken down to Juvenile Detention. I mean, I hurt my mom and dad—emotionally and physically. I didn't punch my mom, but I pushed her, slapped her. She'd get so scared when I lashed out like that. She'd run away from me, or she'd call my dad."

TROUBLE AT SCHOOL

Not surprisingly, his family troubles spilled over into school.

"I ended up getting kicked out of my new school in seventh grade," he says. "What happened was, my friend Jeremy and I snuck out of school and went over to Wendy's to eat. Afterwards, we came back, and the school secretary caught us walking in the door. She told us to go to the in-school suspension room—she had me by the arm.

"I told her, 'You better let me the hell go.' I said that, and more vulgarly than that, if you know what I mean. Jeremy asked her if we could just go, and she said no, we couldn't leave the school. I got mad and said, 'Forget that, I'm going to do what I want.' So she called the principal, and he grabbed me by the arm. I took a swing at him.

"He blocked it, and went running off, maybe to call somebody to help him, I'm not sure. I just ran home. But my parents got called, and because I'd struck out at the principal like that, I was expelled. I had to go to an alternative school after that. Like I said, it was this attitude I'd put on. It was a bad idea, but it was who I was then."

Jorge says that his family tried to deal with the situation by seeking counseling, but that it was not successful.

"I hated it," he says flatly. "I hated being there with my parents, hated the counselor. I mean, he fell asleep sometimes when I was talking! Can you believe that? The whole thing was a big waste of time, and nothing at all was accomplished, except maybe that I was even more resentful than ever."

"I WAS REALLY ADDICTED THEN"

After being expelled from school, Jorge continued to smoke marijuana in larger and more potent quantities.

"I started at this alternative school for kids with problems," he says. "And I started hanging out with a whole different bunch of kids. I met this one girl, Sarah—she didn't live too far from me. I started buying all my weed from Sarah.

"I had a job then, working at McDonald's. So I had money. I had my own little cash card, and I got to keep track of my money. Anyway, she sold me a bag of pot; I remember being kind of confused as to what to do with it. I had no idea what to do with it—I'd just bought joints before, all rolled and ready to smoke. So Sarah showed me how to use a pipe. She sold me one for ten dollars. She even showed me how to use an empty pop can to smoke, if you don't have a pipe.

"Anyway, I found I was getting really dependent on smoking weed by then. I was buying like forty dollars worth at a time, and me and Jeremy were smoking every day. We'd usually go over to his house; I just carried it around with me in my backpack. Let's see—I was about fifteen then, I guess. It didn't matter though. I was happy whether I had someone to smoke with or if I was alone. I was really addicted then, and it just felt good to be smoking."

"I DIDN'T CARE WHAT MY PARENTS THOUGHT"

Jorge remembers that even though he had a steady job, he always seemed to be waiting for the next paycheck so he could buy more drugs.

"One time, I was really broke, and I wasn't going to get paid for a while," he says. "I just wanted to smoke so bad, you know? So I went in this little closet of my dad's; he had these one-dollar coins from like 1700 or something. I mean, they'd been in his family for generations, passed down over the years. So they were really valuable, not only sentimental value but worth lots of money, too.

"Anyway, I took like thirty of them, gave them to Sarah in exchange for dope. She had no idea what she'd gotten."

He pauses a moment. "At that point, my parents started to lock everything of value in a safe deposit box. They knew they couldn't trust me anymore. But you know what? I didn't care what my parents thought. I didn't care that they were hurt because I'd given away something of value. Like I said, nothing was important to me except smoking.

"My parents didn't even know what I was doing with the money at first—actually for quite a long time. I think they suspected, but they didn't know. They found out one night, after I'd been out with Sarah and Jeremy, smoking this hydroponic dope. That means it's grown in water, and it's more powerful.

"So what happened was, I was so high I couldn't even walk straight. I had ridden my bike home from Sarah's after smoking a bowl with her (that's like a pipeful) and the five-minute ride felt like it took five hours. That was the biggest high I'd ever had, and when I got home it was real obvious something was wrong with me, that I was either really drunk or really high. My mom was like, 'Ryan, are you high?' I just mumbled, couldn't hardly get any words out at all.

"That's when they called the cops, the next day. I know they were mad, and worried. But I was mad, too. They found my pipe, and took me to get a UA, a drug test, at the police station. That came up dirty, meaning I had drugs in my system. No surprise to me. And they were like telling me, you can't do that anymore.

"That was the first time my parents knew I was taking drugs. It had been going on for like four years. They're not stupid people, either. So it doesn't ever surprise me that kids can get by with a lot, too."

DEEPER AND DEEPER

Rather than stop using marijuana, however, Jorge began using more and more of the drug. When his paychecks weren't enough to buy what he needed, he found other ways of getting quick money.

"I had no money in my account," he says. "So I'd go out with my new friend Garret—I'd met him in my alternative school, too—and he showed me how to get money. You take your cash card and make fake deposits, and then take the money out right away.

"Of course," he says, looking embarrassed, "I didn't know that they would catch on eventually and I'd end up owing the money. I mean, I racked up like seven hundred dollars in fees from that. After that, I got to stealing other people's cards, finding out their

Although Jorge's parents eventually learned that he was using marijuana, their discovery and subsequent disappointment only increased his desire to smoke.

codes, and running up their bills. I ran up three thousand dollars doing that, just to support my own habit. And when I could, I'd buy bigger quantities of it, so I could sell some and turn a profit. And sometimes, when I didn't have enough to buy weed to sell, I'd sell oregano and tell kids they were buying weed. I didn't worry about them coming after me when they realized what I'd done—this was a pretty no-crime suburb we were living in. In the city, I'd have been worried, yeah.

"You know," he says, "it's funny. When I was first smoking, I thought it was cool; people were like, 'Oh, you're smoking weed!'

And I'm like, 'Yeah.' I used to exaggerate how much I smoked, wanting people to think I was even more cool. But after a while, it wasn't about being cool. I was smoking so much, I didn't need to exaggerate."

"It Was the Coolest Thing Ever"

Jorge's friend Sarah introduced him to another drug within the next few months, and he was impressed right away.

"I'd been spending a lot of money buying weed from her," he says. "And then one day, she gave me a sugar cube. She says, 'Here, try this.' There were drops of LSD in the sugar cube; that's how they sold it. Anyway, I tried it right then, right out on the street with Sarah.

"Man, I was like tripping for four hours—the high was way longer than anything I'd experienced with weed," says Jorge. "I saw colors, everything was swirling around and around. You just can't go to sleep, you know, because there was so much happening—you're really up for it. I thought it was the coolest thing ever.

"I had hallucinations, too. I remember I was sitting on her stairs, and I started seeing them moving in circles around me. I saw people who weren't really there, and I heard voices. The walls of the houses were dripping. It's hard to describe it all. It was so interesting, so different from anything I'd ever done.

"I was ready to do that again, but the second time wasn't good at all. I had a bad trip, it's called—I was really in bad shape. I fell, you know, and it felt as though I were falling forever. I had a real sharp pain in my head, too. I saw things like I did the first time, only it was scary stuff like monsters. I was with Jeremy and Sarah. We were watching a movie on TV, and it seemed to me that stuff was coming out of the TV, right into the living room, right after me.

"Well, Sarah and Jeremy knew what was happening to me. They were holding me down, because I was so scared, so frightened. They told me, 'You're just having a bad trip—you'll have a couple of those, because that's the way it is. But most of the time, it's worth it.' They told me that most of the trips I'd have would be great."

Jorge was not as eager to use acid again after the bad trip. But in little more than a week he felt brave enough to try it again.

"I said I'd do it," he says. "And it was okay—they were right; I had a fine trip. The colors, the moving around, all of that was back. And I knew I wanted to keep doing this, but I got worried later that my parents were going to figure out what I was doing. I told Sarah, what if they find one of my sugar cubes? I asked her if there were any other ways to take acid.

"She got me some stamps—some regular postage stamps—except they weren't so regular in every way. The person she bought the stuff from put the acid on the stamps, on the glue part. So I bought a whole sheet of the stamps, paid like eighty dollars for them."

By age fifteen, Jorge had become interested in mind-altering LSD. Today, he has healthier interests such as playing basketball.

"After a While, I Just Didn't Come Home as often"

It was more and more difficult for him to hide his drug use from his parents, however. When his father asked him if he was still using drugs, Jorge admitted that he was.

"I told him, yeah, I was using LSD and weed, and that I liked it. He was real upset, told me that I had to stop bringing drugs into the house or he and my mom would call the cops on me again."

Jorge was not interested in what his father had to say.

"I told him, 'Yeah, whatever,' and I just kept doing whatever I was doing," he remembers. "I just continued to come in high, do what I wanted. And after a while, I just didn't come home as often. I was using a lot—acid and weed, both of which I was addicted to. I kept my own hours, living in friends' houses, or whatever. I'd go home once in a while, but after a while, my parents started locking the doors late at night, so if I wasn't in by the time they went to bed, I was on my own.

"School was sort of a low priority, too. I sometimes went, and usually I was high. I'd just sleep through classes—no one seemed to care that much. Most of the time I just didn't go though. It was easier to stay away."

"I'd Just Draw a Blank"

Before long his drug use became apparent to his managers at work, and he was fired.

"I'd been at this one McDonald's," he says. "It was just before I turned sixteen, I think. I'd been smoking so much, tripping so much, that it was getting to me at work. I'd come to work high a lot, and four or five times the managers would just send me home. I told them I was sick, I think.

"But after that, they'd had enough. I'd been smoking weed in the bathroom at work, and I was really messed up. I couldn't do things right. Like, the guy at the counter would say, 'Can I get a number one,' or whatever, and I'd just stand there, not knowing what to do. I couldn't focus on anything. I'd mess up on the cash register buttons—I'd just draw a blank, you know?

"So I started working at the Taco Bell right across the street. I needed the money, otherwise I wouldn't have been interested in working. I mean, that's all the money was going for, was drugs."

Jorge says that he was a little more careful at his new job.

As Jorge's addiction increased, his job performance plummeted. Now a former addict, Jorge works at a video rental store.

"I stopped using at work, and I didn't come in high," he explains. "I just waited until I was off work. I was still mowing those two lawns, too, and even with all the hours I was working at Taco Bell, I was getting worried about money."

Jorge points to the stereo on the floor of his apartment.

"See, now I work hard and I buy CDs, radios, expensive stuff like that. But back then, all of that money was going for drugs. And my dad was telling me that I had to help pay for some of the things I wanted to do, like the wheelchair basketball camp, my out-of-town tournaments, that kind of stuff. I wasn't saving any, so I thought, what am I going to do if he makes me pay for those things? I mean, I wanted to do them—I loved wheelchair basketball. I still do, in fact. But there wasn't enough money.

"So I started going back to the cash card thing, or bouncing checks, or even stealing other people's checks. I stole my parents' checks, bought food and stuff with them. I know it was bad, but back then I didn't care at all. I didn't care about anything at all."

"I Had Nothing in My Life"

Jorge was fifteen when his disinterest began to turn to despair. He started having thoughts of killing himself, and said so to a friend, who in turn told a counselor at school.

"I'd been cutting myself, doing that mutilation stuff," Jorge admits. "I was going through a lot of drama in my life, just feeling bad about being adopted, being stoned all the time, being burnt out. I hated my life, I hated pretending I was in control all the time, when I wasn't in control at all. I mean, what did I have? I sat around all day either tripping on acid or stoned on weed. I had nothing in my life at all. I was alienated from my parents, stealing, doing bad things.

"What happened was, after my friend told, they put me in a unit at the hospital. There were counselors there who wanted to get to the cause of my problems. But I didn't want to deal with it. I know this sounds like I'm contradicting myself. But even though I hated my life, I also hated the idea of talking to people about stuff that I didn't even understand.

"My parents told the people at the hospital that I had done drugs in the past. They knew I was depressed, and they hoped the counselor there could get to the bottom of it. But I'd had enough; I was going crazy after sitting in there for three weeks, with no acid, no weed. I couldn't do anything. It was like a prison.

"So what happened was, I just told them there at the hospital that it was all a stunt—that I made the whole thing up, I didn't mean it. I lied, so I could get out. I told the counselor that yeah, I'd done drugs a little, but that I had no problems with it or anything. They didn't know the extent of my use, any more than my parents did. And they believed me!"

To St. Joseph's

After being released from the hospital, Jorge was expecting to go home. However, his parents were convinced that they could not handle him and arranged to place him in a temporary home for children.

"It was called St. Joseph's," he explains. "Lots of different kids were there, for a lot of reasons. Sometimes it was that they had run off, or their parents abandoned them. Some, like me, were there until things got worked out in their families. My parents just didn't want me at that point.

"St. Joseph's wasn't too bad. I did okay there, didn't use anything. I stayed in my room a lot, listening to music. I went to school there, too—you have to, you don't have a choice. I worked hard, too. I had a little job helping with landscaping around the grounds there."

He smiles. "You know, there was one funny thing I thought about there. While I was at St. Joseph's, I spent a lot of time thinking back on things. You know how when you're away from home, you might think about your friends, or fun stuff you did with your family, or whatever? Well, all I used to reminisce about was getting high. I'd think, 'That was fun tripping that one night,' or whatever. It struck me as weird to have my best memories about using drugs. Maybe that's just how it is when you're addicted."

Caught Again

He was released from St. Joseph's after about two months and returned home.

"I tried to live a double life when I got home," he says. "I was giving the impression that I was clean and sober to my parents, but really I relapsed almost right away after I got home."

Where had he gotten the money for his drugs? Jorge shrugs.

"I'd done so much work at that landscaping job at St. Joe's," he says. "And there wasn't really anything to spend my money on there—just their little canteen. So I saved up. I couldn't hardly wait; I bought a *lot* of drugs when I got out.

"But my double life didn't last very long. My parents found my pipe—I'd left it sitting right out on my bed. At first, they didn't want to believe that I'd started using again. They thought it was maybe left over from before I'd gone to St. Joseph's. They were that trusting, I guess. So they let it go.

"But then not long after that, I was over at a friend's house, using drugs again. When I left there that night, I'd dropped my pipe on their front lawn, and his father found it the next day when he was mowing the lawn. They called the cops then, and the whole mess started up again. I denied that I'd been using drugs. Things just went downhill from there.

"I knew that I was going to be locked up pretty soon. It was sort of inevitable. So I took all the money I'd made and bought so much stuff! A lot of weed, a lot of acid. And I was going to use it all—it was unreal. And I didn't care where I bought the stuff, either, and as a result, I got a lot of bunk weed and acid. That's like the stuff is really impure, badly put together. That kind of acid, the bunk stuff, is more likely to give you bad trips. And the bunk weed—well, it was a lot of stuff besides marijuana. Probably like oregano."

He rolls his eyes at the irony of that.

The Fight

November sixteenth was a bad day for Jorge. On that day, he says, his relationship with his mother hit an all-time low.

"I'd gotten kicked out of the high school again," he says. "I sort of was on this back-and-forth thing, getting transitioned from my alternative school back to the regular high school. Anyway, I'd gotten in trouble there. I'd gone out to the Log; that was just an old log sort of off campus where kids went sometimes to smoke or whatever. I went to get high.

"After that, we went back into the school and were wandering the halls when I got caught by a teacher. She told us to go to the crisis room—that was what they called this one detention area. So me and Jeremy went in there, and we were screwing around shooting wedgies [little pieces of paper] around. I threw one at the teacher that was in there, and she called the principal.

"He called my parents right away," Jorge continues. "But I had no intention of waiting around; I knew what would happen. So me and Jeremy started to run. The principal wouldn't get out of my way, so I hit him. We ran back to my house, because I wanted to get some weed I had there—plus my other pipe. My mom was there. She was really mad at me, because she'd had to leave work again.

"She saw I was getting ready to leave, and told me that if I left, it would be the last time. I had so many runaway tickets already, she'd had it. I was mad. I said, 'Whatever.' We really got into it in the garage, and I started hitting her. Jeremy was there, and pulled me off her. The two of us just ran—I had my bike and Jeremy was running alongside of me."

Hitting Bottom

It did not take the police long to catch the boys—Jorge's mother had already called the police.

"I got taken to Juvenile Detention again," he says. "And my parents refused to let me come home. The officers thought about putting me under house arrest, you know, where you have to wear a monitor and can't leave the house? But my mom and dad refused. They didn't even want to talk to me, let alone have me in the house."

Asked if he felt guilty then about what he had done, Jorge shakes his head.

"Not a bit," he admits sadly. "Then, not a bit. I remember feeling more mad than anything else, because I didn't have anybody to call. And nobody to visit me."

Soon afterwards, Jorge was placed in the County Home School, where his parents did come for a short visit.

"They were like, 'Ryan, you know you've really got to change your life around, 'cause you're headed for big trouble doing what you're doing.' I'm like, 'I know, yeah.' Really, I was thinking, 'I'm fine; I don't have a problem with drugs.' I figured I could control whatever happened to me, so I'd be just fine.

"Well, I spent nineteen months there at the Home School. And eventually they kicked me out of there. I refused to go through their programs, that's why. I just sat there while everyone else was discussing their problems. I'm like, 'I don't have anything to say.' I did stay clean for all that time, because there was no way to use drugs inside that facility. But in a way, I felt like I was stoned the whole time I was in there. I just sat there when I was in class, just burnt out, like a zombie. I didn't talk, just sat there. Like I said, stoned without the high.

"So I'd given up. I'd hit bottom—I just didn't care anymore what was going to happen to me. The Home School people were like, 'Fine, go somewhere else and maybe they can give you some help.' They all knew I needed help. But not me. I didn't know it. Or at least, I wasn't admitting it to anyone, including myself."

"I WAS LIKE A DIFFERENT PERSON"

This new treatment center proved far different than the County Home School, says Jorge.

"This was the end of the line," he explains. "It's the place people go when they've been kicked out of all the other places. I didn't have a choice about going here—I got put on a waiting list and as soon as a space was available, I went there.

Now that his addiction and temper are in check, Jorge is able to see how much pain and anguish he caused his family while he was using drugs.

"I started in a CD group—that's Chemical Dependency—and it was run a lot different than the Home School had been. See, at the Home School they had this thing called 'consequences.' So if you're bad, you sit in front of your door—like if you're misbehaving in some way. Man, I was always sitting on a table in front of my door. And in the group sessions, if you can't deal with your problems, you keep sitting by yourself over on a table. Months on end, I was sitting on the table. It isolates you from the group, you see. You're like in a corner, and you can't talk to anyone.

"But in this new place, the people who you talked to were in your group, you know? It wasn't run by the staff so much. Sure, if you messed up, there was a security facility, and you'd deal with the staff then. But otherwise, you were talking to people from like sixteen through nineteen. And it really felt a lot better talking to people like that."

Jorge adjusts the shade on the window behind him.

"I mean, we told a few war stories—you know, like 'When I was smoking up,' or 'When I was doing acid this time'—but just as much if not more of the talk was like 'When I hurt my parents that time,' or 'When I lied to my family.' It really made me think. I felt like compared to the past few years, I was like a different person."

"I Had to Humble Myself"

Quiet at first, Jorge began opening up more and more as the group talked.

"It felt okay—that's all I can say," he shrugs. "It didn't feel uncomfortable or anything. I told about how I'd been smoking every day, and how I was addicted to the weed and the acid. I told them about selling my dad's coins, his heirlooms. I told all about that stuff I hadn't told anyone else before.

"There might have been people in the group who lost a little respect for me as far as the things I had done when I was addicted," he says. "But no one lost respect for me as a person, I'm sure, because I was dealing with stuff and being very honest about my behavior. And what I got from them was the feeling that, like, I could keep talking and they weren't going to shut me down.

"One of the hardest things for me there was thinking about my family," Jorge admits. "I thought about the way I'd treated my mom and dad especially—how I'd been abusive, ungrateful. In treatment we had these things called apology sessions, where you sit down and pretend to talk with your family and tell them how sorry you are. We role played, too, and thought about how it seemed from their perspective, how it felt when I said hurtful things.

"I really felt shameful," Jorge says with emotion. "I felt guilty and shameful about what I had done. And so I talked to my parents—in real life, not just imagination. It was really hard; I had to humble myself. I felt really stupid at first, waiting for an 'I told you so.' But they didn't say that, they didn't say anything like that."

Moving On

After six months in the treatment center, Jorge was released. He did not return home, however, but went instead to a transitional living situation until the time when he could afford an apartment.

"I'm nineteen," he explains. "A lot of guys my age are on their own. I like the independence; I need that. I got a job right away, and I'm working lots of hours. My being off on my own doesn't

To symbolize what he perceives to be a personal transformation, as well as acknowledge his Colombian heritage, Jorge has gotten tattooed and has decided to change his legal name.

take away anything from my relationship with my family. We started getting a stronger and stronger relationship, really."

He looks uncomfortable. "Right now, my parents are very angry with me. I don't know when things will get resolved. See, I got my nose pierced since I've been out of treatment, and also I just got this tattoo."

He opens the top two buttons on his shirt and reveals a colorful Colombian flag with "Jorge" in big letters.

"It's really important for me to change my name back to Jorge," he says sincerely. "I feel like that's who I was born to be. That's what my biological mother named me, and I want to feel pride in that. But my parents think I'm rebelling again, and that makes them nervous. They want me just to be Ryan.

"They won't let my sister talk to me either. See, she's fifteen, and she's just starting to go through some of the feelings I had, about being a minority in a very white suburb, about being adopted. It hurts, though, because the main motivation for me going through treatment was them, and now this happens. It's really painful.

"Maybe things will get back to normal after a while. Actually," he smiles, "we've never really had 'normal' very often for the past five years or so. I really, really hope things will sort out, though. But either way, I know I'm not going to relapse. I'm done with drugs. I did take two hits from a joint when I first moved in here, but I stopped. I thought, 'I don't know why I'm doing this—I don't need it.' So that's that."

COUNTING THE POSITIVES

"Right now I'm finishing my last credit at high school, and I'll get my diploma. I didn't want a GED; I wanted a real diploma. So after this English class is done, I'll be through with high school. After that, I'm not sure. I have some ideas. I'd like to get into management of some sort.

"See, I am sort of a leader, I guess. I mean, a lot of the people here look up to me, come to me for help or advice. I'd like to get into some training at the store where I work, and get as much experience as I can. Then who knows? Maybe I can get into some corporation, do some kind of management there.

"Right now, my basketball team is one of the most exciting things I've got going. I've been doing this for so many years, and it never gets old. I'm a guard on my team, or sometimes I can play point guard. Our last tournament I was the high scorer. Our team is called the Timberwolves, and we wear the same jerseys as the NBA team. We're ranked nationally, too. We're ranked second in the whole country.

"I really miss my dad coming to my games—that's one really bad thing about having this argument going on," he says. "He and my mom have always been the biggest fans. I remember when our team would be playing in Chicago at a tournament, my dad would get up at like three in the morning to drive to the city just to watch the game. He'd spend the day with me, and then drive home that night!"

Jorge looks sad. "Man," he says wistfully. "It was so good to see him."

Jodi

> "I KNOW I'M ADDICTED. I CRAVE WEED, I THINK ABOUT GETTING HIGH ALL THE TIME . . . I'VE TRIED OTHER THINGS, BUT I KEEP COMING BACK TO WEED. YOU CAN'T DIE FROM WEED, YOU CAN'T OVERDOSE ON IT. I'LL CHANGE SOMETIME, BUT NOT NOW."

Author's Note: Except for the body piercing—two centered in her ears and a delicate silver ring on her left eyebrow—no one would suspect that redheaded Jodi leads an alternative lifestyle. She is addicted to marijuana. As she says, "I'm high as often as I can be, and when I'm not, I'm just thinking about the next time." She brings her friend Amanda, nineteen and a self-described "druggie," to the interview, and it is clear that the two are extremely close, with Amanda assuming an almost motherly role.

What is clear almost from the moment I meet Jodi is that she is maddeningly naive about her drug addiction and the seriousness of its consequences. Unfortunately, she seems to have been led down this path by the people she loves the most—friends like Amanda, as well as her own family.

The trailer park is low along the highway, fifteen miles northeast of the city. Jodi's trailer is dark brown, and the mailbox alongside is missing the last two digits of the address. A child's broken riding toy leans against the bottom of the trailer's steps, and a broken screen door hangs open. The inside is hot and steamy, Jodi explains with more than a hint of embarrassment, because the dryer vent isn't working, and the overheated air circulates back inside.

Two women sit at a kitchen table smoking, and they look up briefly, nodding to Jodi. The ashtray in front of them overflows with cigarette butts, and the haze of smoke is like a cloud that has settled in the trailer's interior. The living room is messy, dominated by a hide-a-bed only recently vacated. Pop and beer cans are on every flat surface of the little room. In the next room a television blares.

"We Got to Get Out of Here"

Jodi is anxious to be gone, hurrying Amanda along.

"We got to get out of here," she hisses to her friend, who is moving very slowly. "I don't want to have a big talk about being a druggie in front of everyone out here!"

She turns back to me and smiles, pulling a stray lock of damp hair behind her ear. "We can go to the library—that's like a mile away. I know how to get there; it'll be lots cooler."

As we drive, Jodi explains that part of the reason for the trailer's disarray is that she and her mother have just moved in.

"It belongs to my aunt," she says. "And there's like ten people living in there, and it's really crowded. It's hard to find a place to put any of our stuff. But I guess things will work out.

"We used to live in a trailer park about a half-mile from here. We got kicked out, though—we had too many people living there; that was against the rules of the trailer park. So we're sort of in a temporary situation now, I guess you could say."

"Normal in a Way"

Jodi says that she has not always lived in trailer parks.

"I remember living in some really nice places," she says, somewhat defensively. "Our house down in Missouri was three-story, real pretty yellow. And it had a big porch—really nice."

Amanda coughs wetly. "Yeah," she says, "but you gotta admit—even though you might have lived in nice places, Jodi, your life wasn't really normal."

Jodi frowns. "It was normal sometimes, normal in a way," she insists. "I wasn't always a druggie, you know. We used to be together, all of us. My family is my mom, my dad, and my sister, Jamie. She's ten months and six days older than me. My dad had a job at Precision Tune, taking care of cars, you know? And I did good in school when I was little. I got A's and B's, and I played on

Fifteen-year-old Jodi thumbs through a magazine while at the local library, where she can escape from the cramped living conditions of her aunt's trailer.

a softball team when I was in third grade. I played with Barbies, went to the park, and played just like any other kid."

She admits, however, that she hates school now.

"I don't like to even go," she says. "I have to go to this one alternative school, and there are so many obnoxious, gross kids that go there. So school isn't something I really like to talk about too much. I get good grades—all A's except for Social Studies, which is a C-plus right now. But it isn't hard, compared to a real school. We never get any homework at the school, for one thing. It's just not the same."

"I NEVER KNEW MY REAL FATHER"

But, she says quickly, she is getting ahead of herself. Her childhood was often marred by violence within her home.

"My dad didn't really like me," she says simply. "And see, he's not my real dad, Bobby isn't. I mean, he's the only dad I've ever known, but he's not my biological dad. I never knew my real father. His name is John, and he has red hair like me. That's about all I know about him. Oh, and he is a policeman in Illinois somewhere.

"Bobby, the dad who has always lived with us, is Jamie's real dad. He's married to my mom. But I guess when Jamie was really little, Bobby went off to Colorado to be with some woman. And while he was gone, my mom got involved with this guy John. That's when she got pregnant with me.

"They must have intended to get a divorce, because they both found other people," she continues. "But then, out of the blue the day before I was born, my dad [Bobby] calls up my mom and tells her he was coming home. She was honest with him, told him she was pregnant, but he came home anyway."

Although Bobby's return reunited the family, Jodi feels that he never accepted her.

"We never got along," she shrugs. "We always fought—that was our relationship. I mean, don't get me wrong—he was pretty rough with all of us, including my mom. But it seemed like he hit me more than them. We fought about lots of stuff. When I was little, he hit me for having the radio up too loud, or eating candy. I remember once my sister was eating a candy bar and he hit me, just because I was there. Or sometimes he got mad if there were toys around, and he'd hit me with the belt. And when I got older, it was for staying out too late, or something like that.

"I think—no, I *know*—that the main reason he didn't hit Jamie as much was because she was his real daughter and I wasn't. But back then, when I was little, I didn't know about that. In fact, I didn't even find out I had a different father until I was thirteen. So before that, I used to wonder why he hated me more. But now I know."

She leans back in her chair and folds her arms across her chest.

An Uncomfortable Admission

Jodi and Amanda have been exchanging meaningful looks across the library table; Jodi seems uncomfortable about something.

"See, I've got to say something," she begins uncertainly. "I mean, I love my dad and everything, but I've got to tell you that he was—he *is*—a major drug addict."

Amanda nods her head in agreement.

"He was using drugs probably before I was born," Jodi continues. "I don't know that, but it's probably true. But from the time I can remember, he's been using and selling them. He wasted a lot of our money on drugs and alcohol; we never had money to pay our bills. My mom would have to borrow money so we could pay the phone bill or whatever.

"When he was younger, he was in treatment for drug abuse quite a bit. See, his life was pretty unhappy—his mom died of cancer when he was eleven, and his dad died of alcoholic poisoning when my dad was thirteen. Anyway, he used a lot of drugs, crack, weed, acid, speed. He used crank, too, but only once or twice a week. Probably weed was his number one, same as mine now. Weed is how most people start out, then you move to other things."

Jodi (left) and her nineteen-year-old friend Amanda (right) both acknowledge that they are drug addicts. For Jodi, whose father is also an addict, chemical dependency has long been a part of her family.

Asked if treatment helped her father, Jodi shakes her head vehemently.

"Not a bit," she says. "Not for the drugs, not for the alcohol. If anything, I think it made him worse. I remember one time he was drunk and on crank, and he got really messed up. He got in a bad car accident—he's been in like four really bad ones. We always say that he must have a purpose in being here, because he's survived them all.

"Anyway, he was in the hospital for two days before my mom even found out what had happened to him. When we went to get him, he looked just awful. He'd rolled the car like six times. And when they took out his IV's, you know? Well, he started bleeding again, all over the place."

Jodi pauses as if to emphasize the severity of her father's injuries.

"The next day he came home from the hospital. He was supposed to be resting and everything, but you know what? He was back at the bar the same day!"

"HE SOLD IT . . . OUT OF THE BASEMENT"

She explains that most of her father's money came, not from his automotive job, but from dealing many of the drugs he used himself.

"He sold it out of our house—out of the basement," she says. "I knew all that by the time I was twelve. I mean, you could hardly *not* know what was going on—there was traffic in and out of the house all the time. I'm not sure where he kept his stash of drugs. Down in the basement somewhere. He and whoever was with him would come up after a bit, and they'd look kind of funny, you know. They'd been tripping, or getting high, or whatever.

"I remember when I was little, I'd complain to my dad, once I knew what was going on. I'd say, 'Dad, why do you have to do this? We're going to get into trouble.' He'd tell me, 'Don't worry about it; that's how we make our money.' He wanted me not to worry, but I still did. I mean, who wouldn't worry if their father was doing something like that?"

Her father's lifestyle interfered more and more with their family life, Jodi says.

"He really got into spending money like crazy," she recalls. "He'd spend like $600 in one day at the bar, buying drugs, getting drunk, buying pull tabs. I can't even imagine how much you'd have to use and drink to spend that kind of money! Anyway, that's where our money was going."

Where did her father get the drugs he sold? Jodi shrugs.

"Maybe my uncle. I don't know, really. But my dad didn't have many friends that came over, just my uncle and his little drug buddies. So I would guess it was him."

To Missouri

When she was eleven, Jodi and her family moved to Missouri.

"The explanation was that we were going to move to be closer to my dad's family," she says. "My mom agreed; she thought it would be a good change for us to live somewhere less crowded. And it was okay for a while. But then my father started getting drunk and high even more than before.

"Things weren't so good between him and my mom, either. I remember some bad fights. Sometimes I was right in the middle of them. There was this one time he came home really drunk in the middle of the day. I was home—I'd gotten suspended from school. He asked me what I was doing home so early, and I told him. He got really mad, and he started whipping me around by my hair."

Amanda lifts her head up and interrupts. "I remember *that* fight," she says. "That wasn't in Missouri, that was here."

Jodi shakes her head impatiently. "No, you're thinking of another fight—he pulled my hair in another fight. This time we were in Missouri. Anyhow, when he started hurting me, my mom stepped in between us. He got even madder, and he threw a radio at her. He broke a window throwing something at me, too. It was a beer can, a full one."

Her father was having a number of problems then, Jodi explains.

"He was cheating on my mom, with a friend of hers. And he had a bunch of legal problems, too; he'd written a lot of bad checks and got in trouble for it. He went to jail for two months because of the check thing. When he got out, he right away wrote more bad checks while he was drunk.

"After that they put him in a treatment center, thinking that would cure him. But it didn't. See, like I told you before, he didn't change when he got help at treatment. Like that time, he passed his substance abuse class, or whatever it was called, and graduated.

Jodi (left) says that she started smoking marijuana when she was just eleven, and she had no trouble finding older friends—many of whom she was introduced to by her addict father—who were also into drugs.

Then he came back home and a few weeks later he was back at the bar, getting high and getting drunk, both."

"I Didn't Care at All"

Jodi's own introduction to drugs came when she was only nine years old.

"It was before I went to Missouri," she says. "I was over at my friend's house; we were just sitting on the bed, chilling. She says to me, 'You want to try something?' I told her I didn't care, sure. She told me it was weed. We smoked the joint. It wasn't that great—I got high, but I thought I was going to be sick, you know?

"I started smoking weed regularly when we moved, though. I hung around with the druggie kids, especially when we moved to this town called Trenton. So it wasn't a big surprise that I'd use, too. I didn't think it was that big a deal. I figured if my dad could use it and not be worried, why not me? I didn't care at all, not at all.

"Anyway, the kids I was with always asked if I wanted to get high. I was always the kind of person, well, that couldn't say no to friends. I'd get high with them; I wanted them to like me, you know how it is? So it became a regular thing—I'd get high three or four times a day with them, and so I was pretty much included as much as I wanted to be."

"My Life Became About Getting High"

How could she get high that often? What about school? Jodi and Amanda laugh.

"I had it all figured out," Jodi says. "Me and my cousin Heather would walk to school every day. We'd go into the building and drop off our books and stuff, then we'd go across the street to the house where my friend Dickie lived. Then Heather, me, and Dickie would head over to someone else's house.

"See," she explains, "most of my friends were older. They lived on their own. Most of them were druggies that I'd met through my dad. It's funny, my sister Jamie would be hanging around with the alkies [alcoholics] and I'd be hanging with the druggies.

"So anyway, we'd go to someone's house and just spend the day. We'd head back to school at 3:00 or so and pick up our books, and then head back to whoever's house everybody was at. And we hardly ever got caught.

"We'd have people write notes for us, forging our parents' names, saying we were sick or whatever. And it wasn't *every* day—we'd go about twice a week, I guess."

Jodi says that although she had enjoyed school at first, it became less and less interesting.

"I was missing so much, that when I was there, I didn't know what they were talking about," she admits. "I didn't feel like I belonged there very much, I guess. I was sort of an outsider with all those kids. My life became about getting high with the older kids."

Trying New Things

Jodi and her friends used marijuana and alcohol most of the time, but when she was twelve she was introduced to speed.

"We were at this girl Sammy's house," she explains. "And Sammy asked me if I wanted to try it. I don't really know where she got it, but I tried it. We'd been smoking weed and she told me I ought to try speed, so I said sure. I got three drops with an eyedropper, you know? Right on the inside of my cheek, here."

Amanda raises her head again. "So you got the liquid, huh? You know, it comes in a lot of forms—you can get speed in capsules, in tablets. Jodi, was the stuff you had clear, like water?"

Jodi shakes her head. "No, it was yellowish."

Amanda continues, "It's expensive, too. You get one of those vials when you buy it—five milliliters costs like $105. The vial would last—what?—maybe four months, if you're careful. Lots of times people will store it in those baby juice bottles, you know? They put it in those in their cupboard, so nobody will know they have drugs."

Then to Jodi, she says, "The normal dose for the first time is like two drops, you know. I'm surprised you got three, Jodi."

The younger girl shrugs. "I don't know. But I did. Right over here, on the left side of my mouth. And I felt it right away. It was so strange—you feel like you're just spinning. I felt hot and really, really dizzy, like I was going to puke. I had a hard time moving, 'cause I felt so weird.

"I remember that I stood up and started to walk. I went down the stairs, and then I started to puke. I was scared, but not *really* scared, you know? Everything I saw looked like twice as big as it really was. Looking back, I'd have to say it was more like acid, or crank, the way it affected me."

"I Laugh, That's What I Do"

Amanda is sitting up now, more interested in the conversation.

"You know, Jodi's reaction ain't normal at all," she advises. "On her the speed has a real different effect. Most people *want* to move around—they want to get busy. They lose weight, and get real active and hyper. I know people that will clean their house from corner to corner when they're on speed. But not Jodi—she don't want to move around at all.

"But that bit about puking? That's real normal. That's actually how you know if you got good stuff, if you puke. Crank, crack, speed, whatever. That's how you tell—so puking isn't necessarily a bad thing when you're doing drugs like that."

Jodi thinks of something else. "Oh, I forgot to say one other thing. I was a little bit scared to go to sleep that night—I didn't want to close my eyes. I felt like that a long time—longer than what's normal, I think. It kind of messed me up, that first time. I wasn't real anxious to try it again right away, either. I think I waited like maybe a month before I wanted to use speed again. And after that, I liked it more.

"The one good thing, though, is that I didn't have to pay for drugs very often down in Missouri. Because I was hanging around with a lot of dealers, a lot of older kids who had some money, they were willing to share. Maybe they liked getting high in a group, I think. And we were sure a group! There'd be like eight or nine of us most days."

Jodi says that although lots of her friends seemed more relaxed when they smoked marijuana, she found it hard to stop giggling.

"My friends would also get the munchies—get hungry after getting high," she explains. "But not me, I never got hungry. I laugh, that's what I do. Everybody else is having these conversations, just talking quietly, real mellow, you know? But me, I can't talk to anybody without laughing.

"One time I was with one of my mom's friends, and she and I got high together. Anyway, while we were smoking, I saw this squirrel get hit by a car. It wasn't funny later, when I realized what really happened—in real life. But then, I laughed two hours straight. That's not an exaggeration, either. It just seemed so hilarious to me, seeing that squirrel get bashed by that car."

SEVENTH GRADE THREE TIMES

Jodi maintains that she was able to fool her teachers into believing her absences were legitimate—but not indefinitely.

"They caught on eventually," she says. "I missed so much school, I couldn't keep up with what the other kids in the class were doing. And when I did go, I'd get in trouble. Like I'd run my mouth—that's what gets me suspended most of the time. Not so much to teachers, but to other kids. I get in their faces, start fights."

Jodi grins when I express surprise that she is a fighter.

"You think I look like a nice, innocent kid?" she giggles. "Wow! I'm not at all, especially when some of the dudes at school are giving me shit. Or even the teachers. I got sent one time to the principal, and I'd be cussing him out, calling him real bad names, telling him that the school sucks. A lot of that was the drugs, though. I don't think I did that before I started being addicted.

"So anyway, the first time in seventh grade I missed so much work I had to repeat. And the second time—well, I got expelled right at the end of the year, so that's why I had to go back a third time. And then we moved back up here from Missouri, and I did seventh grade for the third time. And after the third time in seventh grade, they moved me to ninth. That's where I am now. I didn't have to do eighth grade at all."

"A Houseful of Burnouts"

Jodi says she confided in her mother when they still lived in Missouri, confessing her frequent drug use.

Jodi (left) and Amanda (right), along with numerous other family members and friends, live together in the tiny trailer. The two teens freely acknowledge that many of the trailer's inhabitants are also addicted to drugs.

"I know she suspected it," says Jodi. "And she worries about it. She knows I'm addicted now, too. I'm a druggie—so's Amanda here."

Amanda grins companionably. "Yeah, but we aren't burnouts. Burnouts are people who are like doing every drug they can find. We pick and choose what drugs we want. And anyway, if Jodi was a burnout, she wouldn't be doing good in school, and she is.

"I was a burnout before my son Dylan was born. But I'm better now—I'm a druggie. I turn it down a lot of the time. Last night I got high because I'd had a medical procedure, and I was in some pain. But most of the time I do it—what do you call it?—sociably. I'm a sociable user."

"Me too," agrees Jodi. "But it's really hard when you live in a houseful of burnouts."

Both girls agree that the environment in the trailer is not conducive to staying clean and sober, even if they wanted to.

"There's so many people at the trailer—that's the trouble," Jodi says. "If it was just me and my sister and my mom, it would be different. But we can't set the rules, because the trailer belongs to somebody else. Anyway, I don't want to name all the people who are burnouts, but trust me, they are."

"Right Now, This Very Minute"

"Stoner is the biggest burnout in the house," offers Amanda. "He lives there—he's my current boyfriend. His real name is Josh, but everyone calls him Stoner. And my son's father, he's a burnout, too. He lives there. My son's grandma, she uses."

Is it just marijuana that is being used in the trailer? Jodi says no.

"Right now, this very minute, that's probably all they're using," she says. "That's what they can get their hands on in the trailer park. I mean, people sell it there. But if they could get other stuff, they'd do it. I know that.

"What they do is, one will buy a bag and they all share it. Then later, another one will buy the bag. They take turns, I guess. They don't get high in the trailer—they don't bring it in the house. They smoke it outside if it's nice out, or they sit in Amanda's car and get high. It's not like it's much of a secret, really.

"And then there's my mom's boyfriend, Stacy. He was the one with the cowboy hat—did you see him? Anyway, that's weird, because his dad's a U.S. marshal, so whatever he hears, he's supposed to report. So nobody tells Stacy much, no details about what they are smoking, or how they get it or whatever."

IN PRISON

Jodi explains that her mother has a boyfriend now because her father is in prison.

"My mom thinks it's over between them—she's talking divorce," says Jodi. "He's actually in prison in Missouri, even though he was arrested here. That happened last March—it hasn't been that long, actually. How it happened was a lot like that fight I told you about in Missouri. He came home all messed up, on drugs, I think. I couldn't smell liquor on him, so I don't think he was drunk. Anyway, I'd been suspended again."

She flashes a quick smile. "He asked me why I was home; I told him I'd gotten in a fight. Then he started to yell at my sister, Jamie, because our room wasn't clean. Then he yelled at me because the radio was on loud. Then after that, he yelled at me to get up, that he was going to take me back to school.

"My mom told him no, that he couldn't do that. She said, 'I'm not going to let you cause problems down there at school.' He kept yelling, 'Let's go!' I was scared, really. I mean, I sort of just wanted to go with him, just so he'd stop yelling like that. But my mom put her hand in front of me, to block me. But my dad grabbed me by my hair and started pulling me across the floor.

"He hit my mom; I tried to get out, but I couldn't. My mom yelled to me to call the cops, but I couldn't leave. My dad started punching me everywhere—my face, my arms. He tried to slam my mom's face into the cupboard. He was so out of control—really, really messed up. Anyway, we lived above a deli, and so the lady downstairs heard the fight and called the cops. He got arrested and sent to the county jail, but since he was on probation for drug use and writing bad checks down in Missouri, he was extradited back there."

"I'LL NEVER LIVE THAT WAY AGAIN"

Jodi says that her father was sentenced to five years in prison, but that it might be less.

"They're talking about letting him out early," she says. "But my mom wants a divorce—at least she says that. She says she's afraid of the violence, and that she doesn't want to be with him no more."

Amanda smiles. "You *know* they're going to end up back together, Jodi."

"Yeah," says Jodi sadly. "I think so, too. But I hope not. I mean, I love Bobby—he's the only father I ever knew. Even with the things he's done to me. But—and this is the honest-to-God truth—I've told my mom if they get back together, I'll run away. I'll never live like that again, I told her."

Amanda explains, "When I get my own place—me and Dylan—Jodi's going to come live with me. That's all planned out."

"I don't like my mom for certain reasons," says Jodi, trying to choose her words carefully. "She and I used to get along okay, but

Jodi meets with a counselor at her high school, where she says she is able to maintain good grades despite her addiction.

right now things aren't so good. Part of it is that after my dad went to prison I did some running away. She's had me in some foster homes because of my drug use, because of running. I told her a couple of times I hated her, and I didn't want to live with her.

"But part of it is that she's pushed me out, I think. She's spending all this time with my sister. Why? Just because Jamie went and got pregnant, that's why. So she gets all the attention, even though she doesn't do anything. I mean, I go to school, I get A's, don't get pregnant. Jamie doesn't go to school, doesn't work, doesn't do nothing. Gets pregnant. So my mom is real happy, spends all her time thinking about Jamie and the baby. She's overjoyed, that's what she is."

Cartoon Characters and Acid

Jodi sits very still, an angry look on her face. After a few minutes, she looks up.

"When I was doing my running away last summer, that's when I started acid," she says. "That was just like a few months ago. I'd never tried it, but I knew a lot of people who had. It came in sheets, and I took two of the little Bugs Bunny squares."

Seeing my confused look, Amanda explains. "You get the acid in little tiny squares, like a little tiny stamp. They come in sheets, like twice as big as a baseball card, maybe. And there are little pictures printed on the paper, on each tiny square. She had Bugs Bunny, but there are all kinds. Hell, I've had Tweetie, I've seen Rugrats, Simpsons—and what's that guy from South Park? Kenny?"

Jodi adds, "Remember that stuff with the boogie men, the half-clown, half-skeleton? Those were creepy."

"Anyway," continues Amanda, "there's a hundred hits on a sheet, a hundred little squares. And they cover it with this glaze on the top, and there's a drop of acid on each square. Sometimes the sheets are like perforated, so you can separate them that way. Lots of times, though, you have to use a scissors. But you don't want to waste the acid by getting it on the blade of the scissors, so you take the plastic off your cigarette pack, and cover the blades with that. Anyway, you just put the square in your mouth, then, and you start tripping."

"Nothing Looked Real"

Jodi says that her first experience with acid was something she was unprepared for.

"I heard people talking about hallucinating," she remembers, "but it wasn't like I thought it was going to be. Anyway, this guy asked if I wanted to try it, and I said sure. I had been drinking already, and then I took nineteen of these pills. The guy said the pills would increase the power of the acid so I'd get a better trip.

"Like right away, I started seeing Bugs Bunny all over the place. I saw all these little things chasing me, too. The cars looked like they had Bugs Bunny faces, and the streetlights all looked bent over and red. Nothing looked real, absolutely nothing.

"So then I went in the garage, and these guys wanted me to try crank, too. I told them no, that I'd get sick. Then the crank was getting handed to me, and just then I walked out of the garage and puked all over—on my hair, my clothes, everything. I don't know, maybe it was those nineteen green pills I took. I have no idea what they were. Anyway, the high that first time was about two hours."

"THINGS ARE BETTER WHEN I'M HIGH"

Jodi says she has continued to use acid and speed but does not feel addicted to them.

"Maybe I am, I'm not sure," she says. "But I think I could live without them. Mostly it's the weed I couldn't live without. I feel different when I use drugs; things are better when I'm high. I like to laugh, but I don't do that as much when I'm not high.

"Like, me and my sister get into fights a lot. But when I'm high and she says something to hurt me, I just laugh. I don't even try to think of anything mean to say back to her, you know? It's just funny, how that works.

"I haven't used crank yet—and people tell me that's good. So I don't want to limit myself yet. I do want to start on crank at some point, because I want to lose some weight and it's good for that. I have heard that people can die from it, so I'm kind of waiting to see. Maybe I'll get brave and try it soon, who knows?"

Has she had treatment for her addiction? Jodi rolls her eyes.

"It's pointless," she says. "I had to get routine UAs after I started running away, when my mom was upset about me using so much. You just get tested at the courthouse, there. Anyway, I had to go to these outpatient classes once a week. That was my mom's idea—I had to do that if I was going to come home from foster care. So I went.

"But they were stupid! All they did was make me want to get high even more! After each class, I'd run over to my friend's house and like ten minutes later I'd get high. I know that wasn't the idea of the class, but I just was not ready to give it up. I don't think anything works until an addict is ready to quit—look at my dad!"

"I THINK ABOUT GETTING HIGH ALL THE TIME"

Jodi says that she doesn't worry too much about her addiction.

"I mean, I know I'm addicted," she admits. "I crave weed, I think about getting high all the time."

"Me, too," Amanda agrees.

"But I haven't passed the point of no return yet, you know," Jodi says. "I know that weed leads to other things. And I've tried other things, but I keep coming back to weed. You can't die from weed, you can't overdose on it. I'll change sometime, but not now.

"It's not the drug itself I crave. It's the peace of mind. It's the feeling of being really happy, really silly. And I feel that I come by this naturally, if you want to know the truth. I mean, my sister and I both inherited something from my dad—even though he's not my real dad. She got his alcoholism; I got his drug addiction.

"My mom? I don't know. She's not a druggie, no way. I mean, she'll do hash oil once in a while—that's a weed dipped in speed—but she's not into it. She's not the type to get addicted. My dad's the one who's a major drug addict. And sometimes I do worry that I'm going to turn into him, you know? But mostly, I don't think about it too much. I could probably get rid of my addiction if I really wanted to, if I had help. But the honest truth is—I don't want to."

BABY-SITTING HIGH

Where does she get the money for drugs? She grins.

"I don't have to pay too often. Lots of people I know have money, so they'll let me get high off their weed. But yeah, I do buy it sometimes. I don't have a real job, though."

"She worked for me this summer," Amanda offers. "I let her baby-sit Dylan when I was gone at work sometimes. But," she says, turning to Jodi, "I didn't think you were going to use all that money I paid you for drugs."

Jodi shrugs. "It was a good job, though. My friend and I would sometimes watch Dylan together, and we'd both get high."

Amanda doesn't appear irritated in the least. Doesn't it worry her that her two-year-old was in the care of baby-sitters on drugs?

Over the summer Jodi earned money for drugs by baby-sitting Amanda's son, Dylan. While caring for the two-year-old, Jodi says that she and another friend would often get high.

"No," she says. "Not really. I knew she was never really alone when she was watching him. He wasn't in any danger. Just like I don't really worry that my boyfriend now—we call him Stoner—is a major burnout. Because the drugs aren't around Dylan. And the drug use isn't causing any problems between him and me.

"Now Dylan's dad—I had restraining orders on him at one time, because he'd go crazy. He'd punch me, hit me, push me.

Sometimes when I was holding the baby. So I'd get nervous that Dylan would get hurt. That's when I'd worry—not about the drugs, really."

THE PARTY

The future, says Jodi, might as well be a million years away. Her goals are vague at best.

"I might go to beautician's school," she says. "I really like to do other people's hair. Or I might be a cop. I have a record, but no felonies. None of the stuff I've done—run away, drugs, skip school—would transfer over on a permanent record when I'm older. So it might be fun to be a cop.

"The big thing I'm really looking forward to is my birthday this year," she says excitedly. "I turn sixteen, and it's going to be a big deal. I've got my party planned out. I want to get really, really high. And I want lots and lots of weed for presents. I've already talked to some of my friends, and they're all bringing weed.

"Oh, there'll be some other drugs there. I *know* there will be lots of alcohol; that's cool. And some speed, and acid. And I can almost bet there'll be crank. But we'll have the party in a field or something, so we won't be disturbing the peace. But I want to be so high, so drunk that I don't even want to move."

Amanda smiles at Jodi. "And I'm going to take her to some clubs," she says. "Some sixteen-and-over dance clubs. She'll be too wasted to drive—even if she had her license."

"And," says Jodi, "maybe after that sometime, I'll think about getting some treatment or something. But not now—not yet."

Epilogue

In the time since these four young people were interviewed for *Teen Addicts,* there have been some changes in their lives.

Jorge has a new job as a sales representative for a large entertainment corporation. He says that this job is consistent with some of the goals he has set for himself, such as learning management skills. Basketball season is over, and he admits feeling somewhat saddened by that. He and his family have not reconciled yet.

Teshinda continues to study hard and plans to graduate from her high school this spring. She has not yet made college plans, although she says that college is definitely in her future.

Jodi is no longer at her alternative high school—she is back at the public school near her home. Her friend Amanda no longer lives with her. Jodi has a new boyfriend who, says Jodi's sister Jamie, "is the best thing in the world for Jodi—he isn't a drug user himself."

Tyrone has not been seen by caseworkers or friends for two months.

Ways You Can Get Involved

CONTACT THE FOLLOWING ORGANIZATIONS FOR MORE INFORMATION ABOUT TEEN DRUG ADDICTION.

Center on Addiction and Substance Abuse (CASA)
Columbia University
152 W. 57th St.
New York, NY 10019
(212) 841-5200

The center conducts research on drug abuse among youth and publishes periodic reports about substance abuse among high school and college students.

Narcotics Anonymous (NA)
PO Box 9999
Van Nuys, CA 91409
(818) 773-9999

NA offers a twelve-step program that concentrates on overcoming the disease of drug addiction. It publishes numerous informational pamphlets, as well as its basic text, *Narcotics Anonymous.*

National Institute on Drug Abuse
U.S. Department of Health and Human Services
5600 Fishers Ln.
Rockville, MD 20857
(301) 443-6245

The institute conducts research on drug abuse to improve addiction prevention, treatment, and policy efforts. It also publishes a variety of newsletters and fact sheets about drug use by teens.

Volunteers of America (VOA)
3939 N. Causeway Blvd., Suite 400
Metairie, LA 70002
(800) 899-0089
website: http://www.voa.org

This Catholic service organization offers counseling and educational programs for young people, alcoholics, and drug addicts. *The Spirit of America*, published by the VOA, is a curriculum guide promoting the value of youth involvement in their communities.

For Further Reading

John Hicks, *Drug Addiction*. Brookfield, CT: Millbrook Press, 1997. Excellent section on types of people most at risk for drug addiction; helpful glossary.

Raymond M. Jamiolkowski, *Drugs and Domestic Violence*. New York: Rosen, 1996. Easy reading; good chapter on addicted families.

Rhoda McFarland, *Coping with Substance Abuse*. New York: Rosen, 1987. Valuable information on denial and rationalization of drug use.

Lance Morrow, "Kids and Pot," *Time*, December 9, 1996 (cover story). Good information about marijuana's reputation as a "gateway" drug.

Paul Winters, ed., *Teen Addiction*. Current Controversies series. San Diego: Greenhaven Press, 1997. Helpful articles about the effect of pop culture on teen drug abuse.

Index

acid, 8–9
  hallucinations and, 98–99
addiction, drug
  culture's role in, 10
  difficulty in stopping, 8, 12
  home-life factors and, 10–11
  increase of, 8–9
  indicators for, 12
  organizations for helping, 105–106
  paths to, 12
  peer pressure and, 10–11
  reasons for, 9–10
  vomiting and, 92
Amanda (Jodi's friend), 84, 86, 92
  aids Jodi in drug use, 83
  as a burnout, 95
  employs Jodi, 100–101
  explains acid, 98
  restraining order on boyfriend of, 102
amphetamines, 8

burnouts (drug users), 95

Center on Addiction and Substance Abuse (CASA), 11, 105
Cheryl (Teshinda's therapist), 49–50, 53–54
crack cocaine, 9
crank, 8–9, 12
Crips (gang), 47, 50

Donald (Teshinda's abuser), 39–40, 42, 44–46, 54
drug abuse. *See* addiction, drug

escapism, 10
experimentation, 12

Gangster Disciples (gang), 19–20

hallucinations, 98–99
huffing (substance abuse by inhaling), 8, 53, 55

Jodi
  Amanda and, 84, 86, 92
  drug use by, 83, 95, 98
  background of, 13, 83–85
  drug use of
    acid and, 98–99
    baby-sitting and, 100–102
    home environment and, 95
    increase of, 91
    marijuana addiction and, 100
    school and, 85, 93–94
    speed and, 91–93, 99
    start of, 90
  family life of
    father and, 86–89, 96
    mother and, 97–98
    poor relationship with stepfather and, 85–86
  future plans of, 102
Joe (crank user), 12

Jorge (Ryan)
  background of, 13, 59–60
  drug use of
    Chemical Dependency group and, 78–79
    complicates employment, 72–73
    hits bottom, 76–77
    increases, 67–70
    LSD and, 70–72
    relapse of, 75–76
    Sarah (drug supplier) and, 67–68, 70–71
    start of, 63
    stealing for, 63–65, 67–69, 74
    suicidal tendencies and, 74
  expulsion of, from school, 66
  future plans of, 81
  living on own, 80–81
  polio and, 60–61
  relationship with adoptive parents
    anger of, and, 61–62, 65–68, 72, 76
    regrets abuse in, 79, 82
    stealing by, and, 69, 74
    St. Joseph's (home) and, 74–75

LSD, 8

Mara (drug user), 11
marijuana, 8–9
  as "gateway" drug, 11
Marston, Ginna, 10
Marty (drug user), 8

Narcotics Anonymous, 105
National Institute on Drug Abuse, 105

Partnership for a Drug-Free America, 10

pot. *See* marijuana

Ryan. *See* Jorge

sexual abuse, 10–11
Sherman, Kara, 8–9
speed, 8–9, 92–93
Stoner (Amanda's boyfriend), 85

Teshinda
  abandonment of, 43
  angry period of, 46–47
  background of, 10–13, 36
  Cheryl (therapist) and, 49–50, 53–54
  as Crips member, 47, 50
  drug use of
    addiction and, 49
    increase in, 50–52
    start of, 47–48
    suicidal tendencies and, 52, 54
  family life of
    mother and, 37, 40–43, 57–58
    Taronda (sister) and, 41
    Terrence (brother) and, 41–42, 54
  foster homes and, 53–54
    apologizes to, 56–57
    expelled from, 46
    stealing and, 47
  has problems fitting in, 47–48
  progress of, 57–58
  relationship of Donald and abuse of Teshinda's mother and, 39
    drug arrests and, 42
    sexually abusive, 40, 44–46, 54
    stealing and, 47
    therapy and, 49–50

treatment centers and, 53–57
   confession and, 55
Tyrone
  background of, 12
  detention of, 29–30
  drug use of, 22
    addiction and, 25–26, 34
    employment at dope
      house and, 23, 25
    money spent on, 32–33
    shooting and, 26–29
  employment of, 31–32
  family life of
    Clifton (brother) and,
      20–21, 34–35
    Cookie (aunt) and, 21–22
    eviction and, 18
    parents' drug abuse and,
      15–16, 18, 34–35
  future plans of, 33–34
  gang life and, 19–21
  school and, 18

U. S. Department of Health and Human Services, 9

Volunteers of America (VOA), 106

weed. *See* marijuana

About the Author

Gail B. Stewart is the author of more than eighty books for children and young adults. She lives in Minneapolis, Minnesota, with her husband Carl and their sons Ted, Elliot, and Flynn. When she is not writing, she spends her time reading, walking, and watching her sons play soccer.

Although she has enjoyed working on each of her books, she says that *The Other America* series has been especially gratifying. "So many of my past books have involved extensive research," she says, "but most of it has been library work—journals, magazines, books. But for these books, the main research has been very human. Spending the day with a little girl who has AIDS, or having lunch in a soup kitchen with a homeless man—these kinds of things give you insight that a library alone just can't match."

Stewart hopes that readers of this series will experience some of the same insights—perhaps even being motivated to use some of the suggestions at the end of each book to become involved with someone of the Other America.

About the Photographer

Carl Franzén is a writer/designer who enjoys using the camera to tell a story. He works out of his home in Minneapolis, where he lives with his wife, three boys, two dogs, and one cat. For lots of fun, camaraderie, and meeting interesting people, he coaches youth soccer and edits a neighborhood newsletter.